TELL ME THIS IS FOREVER

A BRITISH BILLIONAIRE NOVEL

Book Three

J. S. SCOTT

Tell Me This Is Forever

Copyright © 2022 by J. S. Scott

All rights reserved. No part of this document may be reproduced or transmitted in any form or by any means, electronic, mechanical, photocopying, recording, or otherwise, without prior written permission.

ISBN: 979-8-516234-83-5 (Print)
ISBN: 978-1-951102-62-3 (E-Book)

CONTENTS

Prologue: *Macy* 1
Chapter 1: *Leo* 5
Chapter 2: *Macy* 16
Chapter 3: *Leo* 26
Chapter 4: *Macy* 33
Chapter 5: *Leo* 40
Chapter 6: *Macy* 48
Chapter 7: *Leo* 57
Chapter 8: *Macy* 65
Chapter 9: *Leo* 73
Chapter 10: *Macy* 82
Chapter 11: *Leo* 90
Chapter 12: *Macy* 98
Chapter 13: *Leo* 106
Chapter 14: *Macy* 114
Chapter 15: *Leo* 122
Chapter 16: *Macy* 130
Chapter 17: *Leo* 139

Chapter 18: *Macy* 146
Chapter 19: *Leo* 153
Chapter 20: *Macy* 160
Chapter 21: *Macy* 167
Chapter 22: *Leo* 173
Chapter 23: *Macy* 179
Chapter 24: *Leo* 186
Chapter 25: *Macy* 192
Chapter 26: *Macy* 200
Chapter 27: *Macy* 206
Chapter 28: Leo 211
Chapter 29: *Macy* 217
Epilogue: *Macy* 224

PROLOGUE

Macy

Five Years Ago...

"I'M NOT SURE how to keep going," I whispered, tears pouring down my face like a river as I fisted the grass of the lawn I was lying on, pulling out blades from the soil without even noticing. "I'm not sure I can do it. Please tell me how I'm supposed to go on living without you."

I stared at the enormous wreath made of blue roses, but I heard nothing but silence. My emotional pain was so acute and crippling that I didn't care if it was dark and I was the only living soul still left in the cemetery.

I couldn't leave.

The burial had just taken place today.

My other hand was on a cold marble tombstone, but my heart was buried six feet beneath the soil.

How?

How was the rest of the world still moving on like everything was normal when it wasn't and never would be again?

I wasn't quite twenty-eight years old yet, and my entire universe had already imploded.

I had nothing left.

I had no one who really understood this horrific grief that had left me so paralyzed that I was unable to get my ass up off the grass.

I had no home anymore.

No place to go that felt welcoming to me.

Another round of sobs wracked my body as I remained kneeling on the grass in front of the marble headstone.

I couldn't survive like this.

I couldn't even get up and leave this place.

Was it even possible for a person to feel this much pain and continue to live through it?

I started to hyperventilate as I felt myself losing my grip on reality.

Really, what purpose or value did my life have after what had happened?

Even as I asked myself that question, I saw a flash of possible purpose in my mind, and I held onto it with everything I had.

Wait! I did have somewhere I needed to go, right?

Karma. I need to go see her. I'm supposed to be at the sanctuary to volunteer tonight.

It wasn't like the director wouldn't understand if I didn't show up considering what had happened, but I couldn't let Karma down.

I'd never missed a volunteer day because she trusted me to be there.

Get up, Macy. Go see Karma. You still mean something to her.

I started to take some long, deep breaths, trying to get my brain to function again.

Get. Up.

I wanted to rise, but I couldn't seem to get started.

Get. Your. Ass. Up. Now.

I willed myself to stand, and I stumbled slightly, my knees weak from staying in the same position for hours.

Somehow I managed to get out of the cemetery and make that drive to the big cat sanctuary, doing everything on autopilot until I reached Karma's enclosure.

Once there, I dropped onto the ground, wrapped my arms around the three hundred and fifty pound crippled female Bengal tiger, buried my face into her fur and wept until I couldn't shed another tear.

She couldn't talk to me.

She couldn't give me any advice.

But she comforted me in every way a large, disabled feline could manage, and she listened when I really needed to pour my heart out.

At some point during that visit, I decided I had to carry on for Karma, and because it's what would have been expected of me.

I was a veterinarian and already done with my first year of my zoological residency.

I still had good things to do in the animal world, even if I couldn't face the human part of my life.

My life still had *some* meaning.

I pulled myself together that night and stuffed all of my pain deep inside until it couldn't reach my heart anymore.

If I don't completely acknowledge it, I can somehow live through it.

Maybe not completely facing what I'd lost wasn't the best way of dealing with my grief, but it was my only option if I wanted to keep going.

One day at a time; one foot in front of the other. It was the only way I could function.

I could emotionally shut myself down with a few exceptions.

I had no choice.

If I wanted to keep my sanity, I could never, ever allow myself to love this much again.

CHAPTER 1

Leo

The Present...

"ARE YOU ALRIGHT?" I asked Dr. Macy Palmer once we'd reached our cruising altitude in my private jet. Stupid question, really, when it was clear to anyone looking at her that she *wasn't* doing well.

Macy wasn't actively crying anymore, but her cheeks were still streaked with the tears that had fallen earlier. Not to mention that she'd hardly said a word since we'd boarded.

Bloody hell! I've spent way too much of my time with wild animals in isolated locations. I hardly know what to say to a woman, much less a female in distress who's mourning over the imminent passing of an elderly, cancer-ridden Bengal tiger.

I still had no idea why I'd offered to take Macy back to the United States in my jet so she might possibly arrive there before her tiger died.

Well, maybe it wasn't *her* tiger.

Karma, the aging and sick Bengal tiger was actually Macy's *patient*.

Nevertheless, it was obvious that she was heartbroken because the tiger had taken a turn for the worse while Macy had been visiting the UK.

"I'm okay," she said as she turned her head to look at me. "If I haven't already told you, I want you to know how much I appreciate the ride. I'd still be at Heathrow right now frantically looking for a commercial flight home if it wasn't for you."

One melancholy glance from Macy's serious gray eyes reminded me of exactly why I'd offered to take her with me to the States rather than making her wait for a commercial flight.

She was obviously a woman in emotional pain, and I wasn't the kind of man who could stop himself from responding to that basic human emotion.

Besides, I understood how much it could hurt to lose an animal companion since I was a wildlife conservationist and zoologist myself.

Macy was an exotic animal veterinarian, so I could completely understand why she was heartbroken that Karma was dying. She'd apparently been treating the Bengal tiger for years, and had some kind of history with the feline even before that.

I put my feet up in the leather recliner next to hers as I said, "It was nothing, Macy. Like I said, I was headed for the States myself right after the wedding—"

"But we left before the reception was completely over," she said in a remorseful tone.

I shrugged. "I doubt anyone noticed. The crowd was breaking up, and Nicole and Damian were getting ready to leave."

My eldest brother, Damian, had married Macy's best friend, Nicole, at my mother's country estate in Surrey earlier in the day. Which was why Macy had been in England in the first place.

All indications were pointing toward another wedding happening soon between Macy's other best friend, Kylie, and my other older brother, Dylan, who just so happened to be Damian's younger twin.

Not that Dylan and Kylie were a sure thing. It was just difficult not to assume they'd end up together since Dylan looked at Kylie the same way Damian had been gazing at his bride the entire day.

Dylan had also gone chasing after Kylie like a man with a purpose when they'd had some kind of a misunderstanding near the end of the reception.

My suspicion was that those two would end up engaged in the very near future, if that hadn't happened already.

I tried not to think about what would happen once both of my older brothers were married since my mum could be ruthless in her pursuit of grandchildren.

While I had nothing against marriage in general and especially not for my brothers, I wasn't exactly enthusiastic about tying the knot myself. My life was complicated because I'd always been on the road a lot, and I wasn't the kind of guy most women dreamed of having for a groom.

Well, maybe except for the fact that I was a billionaire from an aristocratic family.

Aside from that, I wasn't exactly marriage material because I was basically already married to my career.

Macy broke eye contact with me and raised her footrest on her recliner. "I still feel a little guilty, even though Nicole and Damian were getting ready to leave their reception. I arrived in England a lot later than Kylie, and I don't want Nic to feel like her wedding wasn't important to me."

"She'd never think that," I told Macy honestly. "It's not like she doesn't understand busy lives and careers."

Since Damian's wife was both a corporate attorney and a business owner, I was fairly certain she knew what it was like to have some very major career commitments.

If not, Damian certainly did. He owned and managed Lancaster International with Dylan, which was one of the largest corporations in the world.

I didn't know a lot about Nicole, Kylie and Macy, but I was aware that the three American women had been best friends since they were children.

Damian's relationship with Nicole had developed quickly, and Dylan's with Kylie had happened even faster. So I hadn't had much time to get to know any of them well.

I'd spent the most time with Nicole, and she was a very easy woman to like. It wasn't surprising that Damian had tied the knot so quickly. Nicole brought out the best in my oldest brother.

I didn't know Kylie well, but I was more grateful to her than I could honestly express. She'd been responsible for taking a very broken Dylan and putting him back together again.

Kylie would deny that she had anything to do with Dylan's recovery, but we all knew the truth. Maybe my brother's tenacity had gotten him through the darkest period of his life, but Kylie's take-no-bullshit attitude with Dylan had certainly helped.

And Macy Palmer?

Macy was basically a mystery to me.

As she'd mentioned, she'd flown in later than most of us in the wedding party, just in time for Nicole's hen party, so we hadn't seen much of each other after our initial introduction.

However, I had to admit that she'd made one hell of an impression.

I'd liked her almost immediately, and my cock had experienced a serious case of insta-love that didn't want to see reason, even though I'd tried.

Yes. Well, I'd tried to tone that reaction down, but my dick was, unfortunately, not listening well.

Admittedly, it had been a while since any female had inspired that kind of bodily reaction, so it wasn't really surprising that I'd chosen to stifle it as best I could.

Number one, it didn't appear that the attraction was mutual.

Number two, she was Nicole's best friend, and I really did like my brother's new wife.

Number three, she was emotionally upset, and who the fuck would mess with a woman who was vulnerable?

I was no innocent, but I wasn't some wanker who tried to screw every attractive woman I met.

Since Macy and I had both been in the wedding party, we'd had a few encounters over the last few days, but the most significant had been when I'd found her crying alone in my mother's library earlier in the evening.

My first instinct had been to back out of the library and let Macy have her privacy since we hardly knew each other.

Unfortunately, I discovered it wasn't in me to just ignore a woman who was crying alone like her entire world was falling apart.

After she'd told me that Karma had taken an unexpected turn for the worse, and that she'd desperately wanted to be there so the tiger wouldn't die alone, how could I not offer to rush her back to the States with me? I'd planned on departing the next morning anyway, so it wasn't exactly a huge inconvenience to leave a little early. I'd have to be a total asshole not to give her the option of traveling with me since I was headed the same direction. I was even going to the same state and general location.

"Really," Macy finally answered earnestly. "My life isn't all that crazy busy right now. It's just the whole situation with Karma. My timing has always sucked."

I wasn't sure she was being completely honest about her schedule, but maybe her idea of busy and mine were entirely different.

Macy was a beautiful woman, but the dark circles under her eyes and what looked like long-term stress was definitely taking its toll on her delicate face right now.

If I had to guess, I'd say that Karma had been sick for quite some time—or there were other things in her life that were getting to her.

"It wasn't exactly *your* timing," I pointed out. "You didn't set the wedding date, and Damian was in one hell of a hurry to put a wedding band on Nicole's finger. I doubt it would be easy for anyone to just drop everything and travel out of the country to be in a wedding on fairly short notice. It wasn't easy for me and I'm my own boss."

If anyone had heard Damian complain before the nuptials, they would have thought he'd waited for years rather than merely a few months to marry Nicole.

A ghost of a smile appeared on Macy's lips. "Damian and Nicole were meant to be together. I don't blame either of them for not wanting to wait."

"Dylan and Kylie, too," I added.

Her voice sounded surprised as she asked, "Do you really think they'll end up together? I mean, I think you're right, but I have no idea how Dylan feels about Kylie. Well, other than the fact that he looks at her like he's crazy about her."

She sounded genuinely pleased about the idea of Kylie finding the right man for her in Dylan.

"I definitely think they'll end up together," I answered confidently. "You don't blame him for being such a wanker before he got his shit together?"

Dylan had been a complete prick when Kylie had walked into his life.

She shook her head. "No. From what I understand I think he had a good reason for going off the deep end. If he's good to my friend now, that's all that really matters."

Macy had obviously missed the fact that Kylie had fled the estate in tears with Dylan following in her wake so he could finally make it crystal clear exactly how he felt about her.

Although I had no intention of telling Macy anything that might upset her more, I saw no reason not to tell her that Dylan and Kylie were mad about each other. It was the truth. "He's in love with her."

She sighed as she rested her head back against the leather seat. "I hope you're right. Kylie so deserves her own happy ending."

Macy sounded so damn weary, looked so incredibly drained, that I wished there was something more I could do to help her.

"What about you?" I asked. "You don't look particularly happy right now. Don't you deserve to be happy?"

She stretched as she got comfortable in the recliner. "Maybe some of us just aren't meant to be committed, married and blissfully happy," she said wryly.

Since I felt the same way, I was surprised that her words rankled just a little.

I'd been attracted to Macy Palmer from the moment I laid eyes on her.

And…I'd been thoroughly surprised that there was no man by her side or back in the States for her, so apparently her single status was by design.

Not quite sure what to say, I finally said, "Maybe you can manage to get some sleep. We're at cruising altitude and the ride looks smooth for now."

She looked completely knackered, so any sleep she could get would likely help her.

"Maybe so," she said noncommittally. "I'm really not all that tired at the moment."

I forced myself not to stare at her but I couldn't quite stop contemplating her single status. Surely there had been plenty of men who had tried to change that.

I doubted there were very many red-blooded males who wouldn't notice Macy.

She had curves in all the right places, pretty walnut colored hair that fell in a silken cloud until it ended in a bob just short of her shoulders, creamy skin that made a man want to reach out and touch her and plump lips that would make a man fantasize about them in any number of ways.

And those damn eyes…

That gloriously expressive, grayed-eyed gaze that seemed to radiate emotion was probably the feature that had really grabbed me by the balls.

I had to wonder if she knew that her eyes were spellbinding and made a man wonder exactly what she was thinking.

I could either read her emotions in her eyes with crystal clarity or they would give me absolutely no clue what thoughts were in her head.

Either way, they were mesmerizing, whether she was an open book at that moment or a mystery I wanted to solve.

When Macy asked a question during a conversation, she wasn't doing it out of some sense of politeness. She really wanted to know the answer, and you could see the anticipation and curiosity in her gaze.

Like, when I'd talked to her about some of my field work to find species that had already been declared extinct.

Granted, she was an exotic animal vet, so it might be natural that she'd feel the same enthusiasm, but I hadn't met a woman quite like Macy in a long time.

I hadn't been introduced to a woman I could talk to who was even remotely interested in threatened species or conservation, unless they actually worked on my field team. Which was probably why I never bothered to talk much about my work when I was circulating in the ultra-wealthy world, I'd grown up in.

It was also the reason I rarely wasted my time on dating anymore.

Most people didn't understand why a billionaire would choose to spend his time tramping through a bug-infested jungle in search of a creature thought to be extinct.

Unfortunately for them, they'd also never know the satisfaction of being part of a team that helped save a species from extinction.

My family understood why I'd chosen to step out of the day-to-day running of Lancaster International and the life I grew up in to pursue my own interests.

Most of the others in that same circle never would.

Because I'd been born and bred a Lancaster, I could fit into both worlds, but my choice was to do whatever I could for wildlife conservation. Especially those species that man's stupidity had put on the extinct and critically endangered lists in the first place.

"Would you like a drink? Food?" I asked, wanting to find some way to ease the look of stress and fatigue from Macy's face.

When she didn't answer, I turned my head only to realize she was asleep.

Not really all that tired, my ass.

Something told me she was fighting off exhaustion a lot more often than she wanted to admit.

Her eyes were closed, her head tilted to one side in what looked like a rather... uncomfortable position.

Bloody hell. She'll wake up with a neckache from sleeping like that.

I unbuckled my seatbelt, and then hers, before I lifted her gently into my arms, hoping not to wake her.

I wanted to curse myself because my cock got rock-hard the moment I had her settled against me.

Christ! It had been way too long since I'd gotten laid.

I barely knew the attractive woman I was holding in my arms, yet her effect on every one of my senses was almost profound.

She felt amazing.

She smelled amazing.

No doubt she'd taste fantastic.

"Fuck!" I cursed again under my breath, thoroughly disgusted with myself.

I wasn't some tosser who got hard every time he saw or touched a female.

I strode back to the bedroom, hit the switch for the soft light underneath the headboard, and put Macy down on the bed.

She had changed after she'd boarded the jet into a pair of jeans and a soft pink T-shirt with the logo of the big cat sanctuary where she worked.

She looked comfortable but somehow, she still appeared to be so damn…vulnerable.

Her brow was furrowed, and she didn't look like she was in a peaceful slumber.

"Bloody hell," I said quietly, wondering what it was about *this woman* that was getting under my skin.

Annoyed, I finally tore my gaze away from her defenseless form and grabbed a blanket to cover her.

I had plenty of other things to think about right now.

Like a possible new discovery in the Mediterranean if some rumors turned out to be true.

Not to mention my new conservation center that I was building near Palm Desert in California.

The new center was the reason why I was going to the US. It was a huge undertaking, and we weren't even beyond the setup phase at this point.

I also had the endless responsibilities of my larger conservation center that was already running in England.

Every day, we had new challenges there with the captive breeding programs.

We'd have those very same challenges in California, too.

I absolutely *did not* need to be so damned focused on a female who was sad over losing a feline friend.

She'd get over her loss, right?

This field of work was full of wins and losses, with more of the later the majority of the time.

"Right then," I said under my breath. All I had to do was focus on the multitude of responsibilities that were waiting for my attention.

They'd make me forget all about the despondent but beautiful exotic vet in no time.

I turned the light off before I moved toward the door.

She'd sleep through the flight.

I could crash on the couch.

Since I slept in some pretty rough places at times, sleeping on the sofa was no imposition for me.

Despite my resolve to only focus on work, a mumbled sound of distress from Macy made me halt suddenly right as I reached the door.

Fuck!

What if she woke up scared?

What if she didn't know where she was because I'd carried her back here?

What if she needed…someone?

I walked to the other side of the bed, resigned, and stretched out next to her.

Since I was the only "someone" available at the moment, I supposed that I needed to stay close to her.

I gave up on any pretense of thinking about work as Macy rolled closer to me and burrowed into my side like she was a heat seeking missile looking for her warm target.

I wrapped an arm around her and was gratified to hear her sigh and then settle down as though she was finally safe from whatever burdens had been plaguing her.

Making certain that Macy Palmer felt like she was safe in her slumber seemed to suddenly be my priority.

At least for now, whether I wanted to do it…or not.

CHAPTER 2

Macy

I WOKE UP SLOWLY, my senses overloaded with unusual sensations.

I was snuggled up against something warm, hard, and utterly irresistible.

A small moan escaped from my lips as I stroked a hand down what felt like a very muscular chest that led to equally chiseled abs.

Annoyed that I had to stroke through cotton material, I searched for and found the edge of that shirt so I could push my hand underneath it.

Since this was my damned fantasy, I wanted some bare skin.

Delighted, I traced every one of the six pack abs I was groping, sighing as I reached the very last one and my hand moved lower…

"Sweetheart," a low baritone voice warned. "If you reach that promised land, I can assure you that you'll get more than you bargained for."

My hand stilled.

Shit! I knew that voice with the sexy British accent.

"Okay, I guess this isn't just a hot fantasy," I muttered as I pushed away from Leo Lancaster's smoking hot body. "What happened? Where in the hell am I?"

If I remembered right, the last time I'd spoken with him I'd been reclined in one of the chairs in the cabin of his private jet.

"You fell asleep," he explained as he tightened his arm around my waist like he didn't want me to go far. "I didn't want you to be uncomfortable, so I brought you back here to sleep in the bed. We're both completely clothed. Nothing happened. We were just sharing the bed to sleep. Well, until you started that interesting exploration of yours. Not that I minded. I just wasn't certain that things would stay completely innocent if your hand kept roving south like that."

"Oh, God," I groaned against his shoulder. "I'm sorry. I think I woke up…confused."

In all honesty, I'd actually woken up in a sensual fog and I'd known *exactly* what I'd wanted.

I just hadn't realized that I was going after the most unattainable billionaire on the planet.

Leo Lancaster was not only one of the wealthiest guys on Earth, but one of the hottest as well. He was a blue-eyed blond with perfect bone structure and a completely droolworthy body that had to be slightly over six-foot tall.

"Don't apologize," he said, humor still vibrating in his voice. "I'd be lying if I said that I didn't enjoy waking up with your hands all over my body. I just didn't want you to hate me later when you realized exactly who you were feeling up."

Like I'd really be annoyed to find myself groping Leo Lancaster?

Holy hell! He *was* the fantasy.

To me, the guy was a legend.

I'd watched every documentary they'd ever filmed on his expeditions, and every videoed lecture he'd ever given.

The man had done unbelievable things in the name of wildlife conservation and the rescue of critically endangered species.

Leo was young, but he'd already been responsible for relocating several species that had been declared extinct.

"How long was I sleeping?" I asked curiously.

"We've both been out for a while. We've only got a few hours left of the flight," he informed me.

Wow! I'd spent a lot of hours out cold next to Leo Lancaster.

I shuddered as I remembered exactly why I was flying home with Leo. "God, I hope I make it in time," I said out loud.

"I've been thinking about that. I'm landing in Palm Springs. I have a home and a vehicle there. I think grabbing my vehicle and driving you to the sanctuary would be the quickest way to get you there after we land," he mused.

"You're probably right," I said with a sigh. "But I can't put you out that way, Leo. You're already being kind enough to bring me to the Palm Springs Airport. I'll see if I can rent a car."

"Not happening," Leo grumbled. "We could be at the sanctuary in the time it could take to rent a car. Let me take you there, Macy. It's really not a big imposition."

I was silent for a moment, but I finally said, "Okay. You win. I really want to get there as quickly as possible. I'll be gutted if I don't make it in time."

At any other time, under any other circumstances, I would have put my foot down about inconveniencing him, but I was so desperate to get to Karma that I didn't.

"I'm sorry about Karma," Leo said next to my ear, the warmth of his breath wafting over the sensitive earlobe.

Shit! Why did he have to be so damn attractive and the embodiment of every single one of my fantasies.

I probably hadn't been the only veterinary student who lusted over Leo Lancaster, but I had probably been the one who had panted the hardest.

It wasn't just the fact that he was attractive, although he was ridiculously gorgeous.

Leo was bold, ballsy, and borderline cocky when he was working, although not in a bad way.

He simply went after what he was searching for with a confident, laser like focus that was almost frightening.

It was that very fixation on his goal that made him so damn successful at what he did.

Most wildlife biologists would probably give up once a species was pronounced extinct.

Leo Lancaster…didn't.

Not when he thought there was a chance that the IUCN could be wrong.

He was relentless and passionate about his fight for critically endangered animals.

Call me crazy—or maybe it was just because I was an exotic vet with the same passion—but there was something incredibly sexy to me about a guy who would put his ass on the line to save an animal species.

I finally answered him, "Thanks. I, of all people, know how stupid it is to let myself get so attached, but I couldn't help myself. I've taken care of Karma since my yearlong internship at the sanctuary, and then I volunteered after that at the sanctuary back when I was doing my residency at the San Diego Zoo. She was a mess when she first came in. Her back leg was mangled. There was nothing we could do. Her front leg healed, but it was never the same. It was weak. She's able to walk, but she never got any of her speed back."

"Accident?" Leo asked.

I shook my head even though it was dark and he couldn't see me. "It would have made more sense if it was, but it was abuse. Karma was raised in captivity. She was with a trainer who adored her in her earlier life. Unfortunately, that devoted trainer who loved her died before Karma came to us. In between, she fell into the hands of some human monsters before she was rescued." Tears started to flow down my cheeks as I finished. "She was so damn confused by the time she got to the sanctuary. She'd been taught that it was okay to trust humans. Her human trainer had raised her from the time she was a cub for God's sake. But all of that trust gained over the years was tested in a matter of a few months. Bastards!" I said vehemently.

Leo's arm tightened around my waist. "I'm sure you helped her find that trust again."

I had, but my success had been hard-won. "It took me six months to get close to her, and another four before she'd lay down next to me in her enclosure."

"You actually got that close?" Leo asked, his tone slightly alarmed.

I nudged him with my elbow. "Spare me, Mr. I'll-grab-any-wild-animal-to-save-it-even-if-it-bites-my-hand-off," I said drily. "It's not like you wouldn't get that close if necessary, and yeah, I probably shouldn't have, even though Karma was raised in captivity, but she was used to being physically close to humans. I think the isolation was actually hurting her because of the way she was raised. She was terrified when she first came to the sanctuary, and she wasn't thriving even though her wounds were healing. I was worried about her."

"So you decided you'd make her trust you?" Leo inquired in an impressed tone. "How did you do it?"

"Pure stubbornness," I admitted. "I spent long periods of time just sitting on the grass talking to her calmly and moving closer as she got more comfortable. Some days were good, some days she still seemed wary. Karma had to be the one who eventually initiated contact again. One day, she finally nudged me with her head, and let me scratch her. We've had a special bond ever since. I'm not stupid enough to not know that wild animals are unpredictable, but my gamble with Karma was actually pretty safe. She was born in captivity, and she can't move very fast. I could outpace her if I had to run for it. She's the only big cat I've ever gotten that close to unless they were out cold."

"So once you finished your residency at the zoo, you decided to work for the sanctuary?" Leo asked. "Did that decision have anything to do with Karma?"

I sighed. Our conversation seemed so intimate in the darkness of the bedroom with the two of us this close and in the same bed. Even though the subject matter was extremely tame. "It did, actually. It had a lot to do with my decision when I certified three years ago. Once I'd passed my certification to be a zoological veterinarian, I had quite a few offers, but I chose to stay with Karma and work at the sanctuary. I'd not only done my internship there, but had volunteered after that, so I knew the facility well, and I didn't want to go somewhere else and never see her again. I couldn't."

Because the additional education and residency to be an exotic vet was so intensive, certified zoological vets were in high demand, but leaving Karma had never been an option for me.

"You obviously like it there," Leo surmised.

"I do, but I'm pretty much limited to big cats. Not that I mind because that's one of my specialties, but the sanctuary is fairly small. Nothing like what I did at the zoo," I explained.

"So, you'd eventually like to move on?" he queried.

I swallowed hard. I didn't want to think about the day when I actually would move on from the sanctuary because that would mean that Karma was gone. "That's my plan," I answered. "I'd like to do something a little more challenging. Working at the zoo as a resident was intense, but I enjoyed the challenge. Enough about me. Tell me about your new conservation center."

There were some things I just didn't talk about and we were starting to wade into that territory.

"There isn't a lot to tell," he said matter-of-factly. "It's much smaller than my facility in the UK, but so far it's raising all of the same challenges. Finding land was nearly impossible, but I finally got the chance to buy a nature preserve north of Palm Springs. We'll keep the area protected and simply add the habitats we need for captive breeding. We're in the process of building an emergency and rehabilitation hospital into this center, too. Obviously, our focus will always be to introduce species back into the wild if there's habitat left for them. I'll be working with some species survival programs already in place here in the US."

"How close are you to bringing animals into the facility?" I asked curiously.

I hadn't heard that he'd be incorporating a hospital and rehab into this center, but it made sense.

"Closer than I was a few months ago," he quipped. "We have to have the habitats just right for the commitments we've already made. I have a team and habitat specialists in place who are working on it. I'm hoping we can start operations and get the rehab center up within the next few months."

"That's amazing," I said softly. "You do some really incredible work, Leo."

"I don't work nearly as hard as some of my team. I don't work as hard as an exotic vet, either" he replied.

"Are you serious?" I asked as I slowly started to move away from him. Being this close to Leo Lancaster was a little too much. "I've seen all of your documentaries and your videotaped lectures. Never have I ever climbed a ridiculously large tree so far up that the fall would kill me just to look for signs of wildlife living up there.

Nor have I jumped into the swift current of a river to get a grip on a critically endangered animal that might die if I didn't. I've also never repelled down into a cave when I had no idea if there was an exit available. You're absolutely insane. You're like the Indiana Jones of rare wildlife. You even have a similar hat. Your lecture videos weren't close enough for me to see the attendees, but I wouldn't doubt the females had love notes on their eyelids. My job is completely tame next to yours."

I kept trying to move away, but Leo obviously wasn't taking the hint.

His arm stayed tightly locked around my waist, and for some reason, I had no desire to keep retreating.

There was no creepiness in his hold.

It was warm, comforting, and it felt like he was almost unaware that he had that muscular arm firmly locked around my body.

I knew I was going back home to heartbreak, so it actually did feel good to be close to someone right now.

I allowed myself to finally relax and rest my head comfortably on the pillow we were apparently sharing, even though I knew it was probably dangerous.

"You actually watched all of those documentaries?" Leo asked, sounding humorously horrified. "Most of them were filmed while I was doing work for my advanced degree, and my hat looks nothing like an Indiana Jones fedora. It's practical. I wear it to shade my face, so I don't get sunburned."

"Okay," I considered. "Maybe it's more like…an outback hat that's slightly lower profile, but close enough, Indie."

"I'm not some kind of wildlife Indiana Jones," he said in a disgusted tone. "I'm not that crazy. I take a few calculated risks sometimes, but nothing that dangerous. I'm still surprised that you've actually seen those documentaries."

"They were interesting," I sputtered.

"They were dry and utterly boring," he grumbled. "But I let a film crew follow me on some of my trips for educational purposes. If I can get some people interested in conservation, it's worth the trouble."

They were far from dull, and Leo was incredibly entertaining. He probably had no idea how enthusiastic he got on film over his research. "They were all well done."

"I'm glad you think so. I'm willing to bet there were very few people who actually saw them," he said wryly.

He might be surprised by how many had watched.

Leo was respected in his field, and just the biologists, zoologists, vets, and other wildlife professionals alone that had followed his career and accomplishments were probably numerous.

Because he liked to share his knowledge and his adventures, he had millions of followers on social media.

Okay. Yeah. No doubt some of those follows were women who drooled over Leo, but that wasn't the only reason people found his newsfeeds interesting.

"You've seen and done more things than I can even imagine doing in my lifetime," I said thoughtfully.

"I doubt that's true," Leo said skeptically. "And I'm not capable of healing animals like you are. I just study wildlife. I don't have your incredible skills to save injured or sick animals."

I snorted. "I think you're just trying to make me feel better."

"Not at all," he said huskily as his head moved closer to mine. "And is it so bad that I admire what you've accomplished, too? Becoming an exotic vet takes intense dedication. And honestly, the travel in my job isn't always exciting. The majority of it is tedious and uncomfortable. I don't see as much of my family as I'd like, and fuck knows I can't hold down a relationship of any kind."

"So…it's probably lonely sometimes?" I asked hesitantly.

"*Most* of the time," he confessed. "So don't envy what I do too much."

It was hard to imagine a guy like Leo feeling isolated, but the brief note of vulnerability in his voice made my breath catch.

Lonely?

God, I knew lonely, and I understood that emotion all too well.

I lifted my hand to his face without thinking as I breathed out, "Leo?" My voice was no more than a whisper.

My fingertips came into contact with his whiskered jaw, and I shivered as I ran my fingers along his rough jawline.

"Macy," Leo said hoarsely right before his mouth moved close enough to kiss me.

CHAPTER 3

Leo

*B*LOODY HELL!

Macy might smell as sweet as honeysuckle, and she probably tasted like sexy sin and mind-blowing orgasms.

But if I got one fucking taste, I knew I *would not* be able to stop.

I was attracted to this woman in a way I didn't even understand, and I had no business kissing her.

We barely knew each other, and she was the best friend of my brother's new wife.

It nearly killed me, but I backed off and resisted the powerful urge to claim those beautiful lips of hers.

Christ! I didn't want to scare the hell out of her.

The insane urge to get closer to her was already alarming the hell out of *me*.

I didn't feel the need to screw every attractive woman I encountered.

Yes, I liked to get laid as much as the next guy, and I did get laid. *On occasion.*

I'd just never felt sexual chemistry quite like...this.

There wasn't just a spark of interest with Macy.

It was a raging inferno that I could hardly contain right now.

"I don't," she murmured quietly.

"Don't what?" I asked hoarsely.

"Totally envy what you do," she said, answering back to my earlier warning. "I mean, yeah, I'd love to travel and see animals in their natural habitat, but there's a certain satisfaction in spending time with the same animals. Watching their progress. Following everything through until they're back on their feet and healed. I can't save them all, but I rehabilitate enough of them to recognize that I make a difference."

She made an enormous difference, but I also realized that her occupation took a toll on her.

It wasn't always possible for someone with a heart to keep their distance in her job, and it was obvious that Macy put her entire heart into her patients.

"You'll get to do that traveling one day," I told her. "You're incredibly young—"

"Older than you are. I'm pretty sure," she said lightly.

"Not possible," I shot back. "Age?"

"Thirty-three just a few weeks ago. You?"

"Thirty-two six months ago. So, you aren't even a year older than I am," I informed her.

"You're definitely a lot more worldly than I am," she bantered.

"If by that you mean that I've seen more of the world, you're probably right, but most of my time spent around the world was in the pursuit of research. I haven't gone sightseeing since I was a kid. What countries have you checked off your wish list so far?" I asked curiously.

"Not many," she confessed. "Canada and Mexico. But a lot of Americans have been over the border of those countries. When I was a teenager, I went to the UK and a few countries in Europe, and of course I was just recently back in England. Unfortunately, I've never been anywhere with interesting wildlife, unless you want to count the drunk college kids on spring break in Mexico."

"You've spent most of your adult life training to be an exotic vet," I reminded her. "Give it some time."

"I'll eventually get to the places I want to go," she said in a lighter tone. "So how long are you hanging out in the US this time?"

"I'll be here for a while," I explained. "That's why I bought a home near the conservation center. I know from experience that the first year or so of setting up the breeding programs are a challenge. I'm getting a great team in place, but I'd like to be here to supervise the process in the beginning."

"That makes sense," she mused. "Seeing as you've been through this whole setup process before. No more trips into the wild?"

"Something could come up," I shared. "All I have are rumors and a few sightings right now, but I've heard that the eyewitness accounts are probably reputable. It's possible that there could still be a few Lanian lynxes in existence."

She was quiet for a moment before she whispered, "No way. Are you serious? They were put on the extinct list over a decade ago."

"The country was involved in a civil war for a very long time," I told her. "The Lanian rebels lived and hid on the remote side of the island nation. Their occupation of that area messed with the entire ecosystem. There were far too many rebels living off the meager resources there. The Lanian lynx suffered because of it. The rebel armies nearly wiped out the rabbits in the area, which were the lynx's main source of food. Once the rabbits were nearly gone, the lynxes were hunted for food, too. It would be surprising if there are any left, but apparently the ecosystem is starting to recover now that the area isn't occupied."

"It would be a miracle," Macy said in an awed tone. "The Iberian lynx was at the brink of extinction, and it's still endangered, but the numbers are improving. It would be amazing to find another species of lynx that we thought was completely lost."

"Don't get too excited. It's just rumor and some unsubstantiated evidence," I told her. "The civil war has been over for years, and that area in the north is pretty remote now, so it's possible that a population still exists, but not probable."

"So, most of the humans are gone?"

"They are," I confirmed. "The majority of the human population is in the south on the coastline, near the capital city. Southern Lania is now a fairly popular tourist destination for people who love the beach. The north is a harsher environment. It's mountainous in the far north. Mostly small fishing villages here and there, and an occasional farm until you get to the foothills."

"I'm sure it's beautiful there," Macy said. "It's located in the middle of the Mediterranean. So, do you think you'll go investigate if you can get more information?"

"I'm already on it. I've even spoken to Crown Prince Niklaos, the ruling monarch. Nick, Dylan and Damian were actually mates at university. I didn't know him quite as well as my brothers, but he seemed nice enough. Nick is requesting that I explore there for the lynx if we get some more concrete proof that they may still exist there. He's sending some of his biologists up north to do some basic scouting."

"Wait!" she exclaimed. "Are you telling me that you're actually buddies with a crown prince?"

"Not exactly," I explained. "Like I said, Nick was friendlier with my brothers. Are you familiar with the beach house that Dylan recently bought in Newport Beach?"

"Yeah," she said in a reverent voice. "That fantastic place that sits right on the beach."

"That's the one," I agreed. "That place belonged to Nick at one time. He bought it when he returned to his royal duties in Lania, but he didn't get to the States very often. I think he was probably glad that Dylan decided to buy it from him."

"Returned to his duties?" she asked. "I admit that I don't know a whole lot about Lania other than the fact that it's an island nation that was involved in a revolution for a long time. Wasn't Prince Niklaos born there if he's a crown prince?"

"Long story," I replied. "He was born there but was sent to England for his safety as a child to protect the royal line during the civil war. He only returned to his own country once the rebellion was over and his father became too demented to rule."

"That must have been extremely overwhelming for him if he's only Dylan and Damian's age," she pondered. "I guess no one really knows what responsibility means until they have to run an entire country that's been a war-torn mess for decades. I can understand why entire ecosystems were wiped out there."

"He's done a good job at restoring Lania so far," I admitted. "They don't have the resources and all of the technology that the UK and US have, but he's working on it. Turning the south into a tourist mecca was probably a great idea. It will bring in the funds to do all of the reconstruction that needs to be done."

She sighed. "I'd love to hear how it turns out and what they find there."

"You will hear about it," I replied. "I'm not about to lose touch. I'd like to show you around the conservation center if you have the time to come visit."

Did she think I was just going to dump her back home and never talk to her again?

That wasn't happening.

Palm Desert wasn't that far from Newport Beach.

I remembered that Nicole had once told me that she, Kylie and Macy were really close because they'd been friends since grade school. She'd also mentioned that since none of them had any other family in California anymore that they were tight like sisters.

Nicole was on her honeymoon, and Kylie was still in the UK with Dylan. I had a feeling Kylie probably wasn't coming back to the US anytime soon if Dylan had any say in her return date.

So, who in the hell was going to be there for Macy right now?

Granted, my priority was generally my work, but that didn't mean I didn't understand that Macy was going to need a friend to help her get through losing Karma.

"I'd like that," she murmured. "I feel lucky to get an invitation. Everyone will be vying for one."

"Consider it an open invite to come to Palm Springs any time you want. I have a large home and you're always welcome. I doubt I'll be away much. For now, my priority is the conservation center and writing papers for some of my research. I haven't published in a while, and there's some important data I'd like to get out there," I explained. "If I can't sell you on visiting at this time of the year, I doubt I'd get you out there in the middle of summer."

"I do live in Southern California," she reminded me. "I'm used to the heat, but the Palm Desert area is so hot. I don't think it will really cool down until winter."

"I have a nice pool and air conditioning," I joked.

"Of course, you do," she teased back. "And you're right. The weather is improving there now that we're going into fall. I'll definitely be out for that visit."

I hated myself because I was hoping there would be more than one visit.

"I'm hoping you'll consider me a friend you can talk to if you need me," I told her.

She was silent for a moment before she answered, "Things will be kind of weird with Nicole living in the UK now, and I know there's something going on with Kylie and Dylan. So I'm not sure when she'll be back, either. Not that any of us will lose touch. We've had geographic challenges before and our friendship never changed. It's just going to be different now that we aren't all living in the same place anymore or getting together in person very often."

"I won't be far away," I reminded her.

Christ! Could my eagerness to see her again be any more obvious?

"I appreciate everything you've done for me," she said in a sincere tone. "But you're a busy guy."

"I'll never be so busy that I don't have time to be a friend if you need one," I told her.

"Thanks, Leo. We'll see. Thanks for offering," she said in a non-committal tone.

It wasn't a promise that she'd call me if she needed to talk, but for now, it would have to be enough.

CHAPTER 4

Macy

"I THINK YOU'RE PROBABLY thoroughly pissed, Macy. Are you sure you'll be alright alone here?" Leo asked two nights later with concern in his tone.

I stumbled into my small apartment with Leo's hand firmly around my upper arm, so I didn't go face first into the floor.

I'd heard the term *pissed* in the UK enough times to realize that it meant *drunk*.

Was I really plastered?

Okay, I wasn't exactly sober, but if I was *thoroughly pissed* I probably wouldn't be standing right now.

"Of course, I'll be okay," I assured him. "I do live here."

"That's not what I meant and you know it," Leo said lightly as he sat me down at my small kitchen table and searched in the cupboards until he found a glass, which he promptly filled with water and ice.

"Hitting the bar was your idea," I reminded him. "I told you that I was a lightweight. I've never had the time to get drunk. Once in college, and after that hangover, I was done."

Leo sat the water in front of me. "Drink," he instructed. "And eat something in the morning."

"I'll be fine," I muttered against the rim of the glass before I took a sip of the water, knowing I was a liar.

I wasn't fine.

Maybe Leo had suggested a table at a quiet little local bar for some drinks, but I'd been completely on board.

Karma had died late in the afternoon, after lingering far longer than I thought she would.

Leo had stayed with me at the sanctuary the entire time, even though I'd told him to go.

Leo helped himself to some water and sat across from me. "I can see why you like working at the sanctuary. It might be small, but the staff seems to care a great deal about every single animal under their care."

I nodded slowly. "They do."

"The director seemed to understand how difficult Karma's death was going to be for you. He did mention that he didn't want to see your face until next week. In a nice way, of course," Leo said.

"I'm glad he said that" I told Leo as I looked at him over the rim of my water glass. "I'm not sure how long it will take for me to get over Karma's enclosure being empty."

I'd cried like my entire world was ending after Karma had taken her last breath, and Leo had been there to lend a shoulder to cry on.

"Take the time off," Leo suggested. "You need it, Macy. You were there for forty-eight hours with very little sleep. You deserve some time to get through the pain of losing her. I'm glad I got to see the bond between the two of you. It was pretty special and unusual."

I'd kept Karma well medicated for her pain, but there had still been times when she'd been well aware of her surroundings.

"She liked you," I told him sadly. "You have a gift, Leo. Karma didn't trust very many people."

"She only tolerated me being there because she knew it was okay with you," he explained. "Honestly, it was a surreal experience for me. I've never been that close to any of the tiger species when one of them was actually awake. We don't have any at my conservation center in England, and I doubt I'll ever have a chance to hang out with another big cat like that."

"I doubt I will, either" I replied. "Karma was special because she was raised by humans. Most big cats stay wary of humans, and they're too wild to sit and chat with when they're in a zoo or rehabbing."

"So, what will you do with your time off?" he asked quietly.

"I'm not quite sure," I said honestly. "I'll probably spend some time at the shelter where I volunteer here in Newport Beach."

"You do volunteer work at a regular shelter?" he asked, sounding surprised.

I shrugged. "Why not? I've known how to treat regular domestic animals since I graduated from vet school seven years ago. Although that particular shelter is starting to get what you Brits might call… posh. Both of your brothers donate generously to that shelter now, so we're not nearly as needy as we were. They're good men. Neither one hesitated to start writing checks the moment they knew that the animal shelter needed the donations."

"I'd be happy to donate—"

I held up a hand as I said, "God, no. We already get plenty of money from Dylan and Damian, and they both set up ongoing donations. We've been able to take on more animals, and we're no longer in desperate need because of your brothers' generosity."

"Well, the invite to come visit me in Palm Springs is still open," he reminded me.

Like he has nothing better to do than tour me around his conservation center after spending the last two days with me on death watch for a Bengal tiger?

He was Leo Lancaster for God's sake.

He was a rock star of the wildlife world.

I hadn't had enough cocktails to make me forget who had been at my side during the last few absolutely horrible days for me.

Leo had stayed right next to me and hadn't batted an eye over the idea of hanging out up close and personal with Karma, petting and comforting the gigantic feline until she'd passed.

Nor had it been the least bit awkward when Leo had opened his arms for the grieving vet that had been left behind once Karma was gone.

When Leo had suggested drinks on the way home, I was all over that idea.

Of course, he probably hadn't expected me to polish off so damn many cocktails, but he never said a word.

He'd simply helped me out to his Escalade once I was ready to leave and driven me back to my apartment.

I glanced at the kitchen clock and realized it was midnight. "You can go, Leo. Really. I was a little tipsy, but I'm feeling better now. I know you have a lot of work to get done. The fact that you stayed with me for so long means the world to me."

He shrugged. "It was nothing. Is that my cue to get the hell out of here?" he asked jokingly.

"That wasn't a brush off," I said honestly. "I just feel guilty because you've spent every moment of the last few days with me. That's not why you're here in the States, and you haven't even been to your conservation center yet."

"It is getting late," he said in a more somber tone as he got up. "And neither one of us got much sleep last night."

He sounded tired, and as my alcohol induced fog continued to clear, I realized I couldn't possibly let Leo go home tonight.

Most of my emotional energy had been focused on Karma for the last two days.

Leo had been there to bring me food when it was time to eat and lend me some of his strength when I'd fallen apart.

I sighed as I realized I hadn't once thought about the fact that Leo was human, too.

"It's almost a two-hour drive to Palm Springs," I reminded him as I rose from my chair. "You have to be exhausted."

"That's why I skipped the alcohol and opted for a strong cup of coffee at the bar instead," he said as he turned to face me after I'd followed him to the door. "I'll be fine, Macy. I'm used to not getting much sleep when I'm out in the field. I'm still perfectly functional. I'm more concerned about your well-being at the moment. You look completely knackered," he said in a low baritone. "Get some sleep and take care of yourself."

I looked up at Leo and released another long sigh.

Even after two days of keeping company with a dying tiger and a woman who was wallowing in sorrow, Leo looked as good as he had on the plane ride across the pond.

How did a woman thank a guy she hardly knew for being there during a traumatic experience for her? "Leo, I'm not sure how to thank—"

"Then don't because you've already thanked me fifty times or so," he interrupted in a teasing tone. "I know it's going to take a while to get over losing Karma. If you really want to thank me, stay in touch and let me know how you're coping."

I threw myself into his arms for the umpteenth time in the last few days, an action that had gotten easier and easier to do.

Maybe because I knew that for some reason, Leo got me. He wasn't going to judge me. He understood how I felt, when so many other people wouldn't.

Honestly, how many people in the world would comprehend how badly my heart was breaking over a crippled Bengal tiger that had become my third best friend over the years?

Would they understand why I felt so empty and lost?

Probably not.

But Leo seemed to both empathize and sense exactly how I was feeling.

"I'm not sure what I would have done without you during the last few days," I told him in a shaky voice as I hugged the crap out of him.

He pulled back and kissed my forehead like I was his little sister before he answered, "I'm glad you didn't have to do it without me."

"Me, too," I whispered as I inhaled Leo's deliciously masculine scent that I'd come to recognize very well over the last few days.

"Hey," he said in a sympathetic tone as he swiped a tear from my cheek. "Macy, I'd be happy to stay if you need—"

"No! I'm home, Leo. I'm okay," I said as I moved back to swipe the moisture from my cheeks. "I can't keep crying like this forever. I'll find my balance." *Eventually.*

It would probably be easier to lick my wounds alone, but strangely, it hadn't been all that difficult to let loose with Leo, either.

It wasn't like I hadn't lost animals I cared about before. It was the difficult part of my job, and I mourned every one of those creatures to some extent, but never like this.

Karma had been different.

I'd let myself get way too close for way too long, and it was excruciatingly painful because of that.

We'd comforted each other when we were both going through the darkest times of our lives and letting go of her had felt like I'd entered that inky blackness all over again.

"I'll be in touch even if you aren't," Leo warned me as he finally let me go. "I'll have to know that you're alright."

I tried to shoot him a small smile. "You're kidding, right?" I said. "You gave me an invite any zoological veterinarian would kill to get. I'll call you."

Leo lifted a brow. "It wasn't a professional invitation. Maybe I just really want to see you again."

I snorted. I couldn't help myself. "In that case, I'd really consider myself fortunate. You are the legendary Leo Lancaster."

I couldn't say all of my hero-worship had completely worn off, but I didn't quite see Leo in the same way I had a few days ago.

He was still breathtakingly gorgeous and somewhat larger than life, but he was also very…human.

He grinned as he opened the door. "Not exactly what I was hoping for but I'll take that…for now."

He didn't say another word as he departed. As I watched his large, bulky figure disappear into the darkness, I was curious about what Leo Lancaster had actually wanted to hear.

CHAPTER 5

Leo

"HOW IS IT that I knew nothing about all this?" my brother Dylan asked the next day as we caught up with each other by phone. "I've tried to call you a few times since you left the UK, but I'm so used to you being out of touch and calling when you're able that I didn't think much about you not answering."

I'd shared what had happened with Macy after Dylan had let me know that everything was fine now between him and Kylie.

My brother had asked Kylie to marry him the night of Damian and Nicole's reception, so I'd been right. There was another Lancaster wedding that was going into the planning stages.

"I think you had more important things to think about," I answered. "And I just started returning my phone calls. You're the first person I called. I shut my phone off once we got to the infirmary at the animal sanctuary."

"How is Macy doing?" Dylan asked, his tone solemn. "Kylie mentioned that Macy was upset because the tiger was sick and dying, but I didn't know the whole story. I didn't realize she'd been caring for the tiger for so long or how bonded she was to Karma."

I smiled as I stood at the floor to ceiling windows of my new home, staring out at the desert landscape.

Only months ago, Damian and I had wondered whether or not Dylan still had a heart.

The concern in his voice now when he'd asked about Macy was solid proof that the big organ was still beating inside Dylan's chest.

I'd be forever grateful to Kylie for giving the old Dylan back to our family, and I was damn happy she'd be joining our family permanently by marrying my brother.

"Obviously, she was heartbroken," I told him. "She says she's doing alright, but I think it will take a while for her to get over it. It was evident that she and that tiger were really bonded."

"Kylie mentioned once or twice that Macy hasn't had it easy," Dylan pondered. "Now I wish I would have asked her exactly what she'd meant by that. Her educational path was obviously grueling and difficult, but I have a feeling there's more to it than that."

I suspected that Dylan was right, but I had no real reason *why* I believed that.

It was...instinct.

A sense that Karma wasn't the only thing troubling Macy.

"She's looked exhausted from the first time we met, and that hasn't changed much," I shared with Dylan. "I'm hoping she finally got some sleep last night after I dropped her off at home."

"So what exactly is going on between you two?" Dylan asked. "It's not like you to put your own work aside completely for two days, dying tiger or not. I know you're there in the States for your new center and you can hardly be still for five minutes if you have some kind of work you need to do."

I ran a frustrated hand through my hair. "Nothing is going on between us," I assured him. "She needed some help and I helped her out."

"That's complete bullshit, brother," Dylan said with humor in his tone. "Let's hear the real story."

I let out an exasperated breath. "I like her. I can't help myself. But she has absolutely no interest in exploring any kind of relationship with me. I had to convince her to let me take her to Karma and then let me stay with her at the sanctuary. The only reason she agreed was because it was the fastest way to her beloved tiger. She only seems minimally interested in coming to visit in Palm Springs. Any enthusiasm she has is more about visiting the conservation center than seeing me again."

"And…you'd rather she was interested in you?" Dylan asked curiously. "I mean, that's not really like you, either, Leo. When have you cared whether or not a woman was impressed by you?"

"Since I met *her*, apparently," I answered drily. "Honestly, she's different from any other woman I've ever known. I've thought so since the moment we met. Hell, maybe I'm just attracted to her because she's gorgeous. I don't know." I thought about my words for a moment before I added, "Nah. It's more than that. I really want to spend some time with her. Get to know her better. Macy is kind and brilliant besides being beautiful, but she didn't seem too interested in doing anything with me."

"Maybe it's just because her head isn't in a good place right now," Dylan suggested.

"I thought about that, too," I confessed. "But I wasn't exactly sensing any personal interest at the wedding, either. Bloody hell! She's the first woman I've really been attracted to in a long time, and it's obvious that interest isn't reciprocated. She treats me like…a casual friend."

It wasn't like I hadn't been looking for some kind of interest other than friendship from Macy.

I just hadn't seen it before or after our trip back to the States.

"You might just have to be patient, Leo. And for fuck's sake, whatever you do, don't make her a one-nighter and then take off on one of your extended explorations. Kylie will cut your balls off if you hurt Macy. Worse yet, she'll probably cut my balls off, too, since you're my brother. I think she's really hoping that Macy will find herself a nice guy someday soon."

"And I wouldn't qualify?" I asked drily, more than a little offended.

"Come on, Leo," Dylan drawled. "When was the last time you had a girlfriend or anything long-term? I know you aren't a thirty-two-year-old virgin, so I have to assume most of your liaisons were…brief."

"Not always by choice," I grumbled. "Most women don't understand why I do what I do when I have so much money that I could just donate to the cause instead of doing it myself and getting my hands dirty."

I wasn't about to tell my older brother just how infrequently those one-nighters happened.

Dylan let out a long breath before he asked, "What about finding a female who has some of the same goals you do? A team member? Someone who works in your field?"

"Every female team member I have is already married. It's the same for most of the women in this field. I'm looking for advanced education and some experience when I hire someone. If a female on my team or working at the center isn't married, which doesn't happen that often, there's just no…spark. Ideally, it would be nice to meet someone in the same field, but most of the women I associate with are already taken."

"Bloody hell, Leo, you really need to get out of the wilderness more often," Dylan remarked.

"If I do, I start running into the women who don't understand my choice of career," I told him.

"Alright, I get it. It's not like I don't understand how difficult it is to meet the right woman," Dylan said, sounding resigned. "Just... be careful with Macy."

"Did it ever occur to you that *she* could end up breaking *my* heart?" I asked wryly.

"Nope," Dylan replied succinctly. "I know you, little brother. With the exception of Mum, I doubt there's any woman who will keep your attention for more than an evening."

I was tempted to tell him how wrong he was, and that I truly was captivated with Macy, but I wasn't sure he'd believe me. Hell, I probably wouldn't have believed that Dylan was really in love with Kylie had I not seen the two of them together after he'd fallen.

"Thanks," I said testily. "That makes me sound like a complete wanker."

"That isn't what I meant," Dylan said calmly. "You're incredibly driven. You always have been. I admire that about you. When you have your mind set on accomplishing something, you get tunnel vision. That's why you're so damn good at what you do, but it doesn't leave much room for anything or anyone else in your life. That's what worries me. At some point in the future, I do think you're going to want...more. It's not a criticism, Leo. It's just an observation. Have you ever had a real relationship? I don't really remember you bringing a woman home to meet the family."

"None of us really brought a woman home to meet Mum because we knew she'd start planning the wedding," I reminded him. "I had a few steady girlfriends when I was at university. One when I was eighteen, and then a different one when I was twenty-one," I recalled.

"And after that?" Dylan asked, probing for more information.

"So, there was nothing long-term after things ended with my second girlfriend at uni," I admitted unhappily. "That doesn't mean I didn't want a relationship. It just…didn't happen. Look at Damian. He didn't have a woman in his life for a long time, either. Not until Nicole."

"Then I guess there is still hope for you," Dylan joked. "I'm just asking you not to mess with Macy. She's one of Kylie's best friends."

"What if she's the woman who makes me want more?" I challenged.

It wasn't like I felt this way about a woman every bloody day.

"Then fuck it if you're really crazy about her," Dylan said flatly. "You go for it. Nothing in life is guaranteed. I learned that the hard way."

"Honestly," I confessed. "I'm not sure exactly what I'm going to do. I'm attracted to her. I'm not going to lie about that. But it's more than that. I want a lot more than a one night stand."

"Are you going to call her?" Dylan asked curiously.

"I was hoping she'd call me," I told him. "I made it very clear that I wanted her to call, and that I was embarrassingly eager to hear from her."

"Don't hold your breath," Dylan answered. "If she's as stubborn as Kylie, she'll be capable of holding out way longer than you wanted to wait to see her again."

He was probably right.

Something told me if I didn't hear from Macy soon, I'd be the one calling her. There was something about the chemistry between the two of us that I just couldn't ignore.

Bloody hell! Maybe it would be better if I just brushed off the whole situation with Macy, but I wasn't sure if I could.

"Things could get really complicated," I informed Dylan.

"How so?"

"Macy is a very talented zoological vet and I'm a guy who's opening a conservation center, an emergency wildlife hospital and a wildlife rehab center. It's damn hard to find a good exotic animal vet, and now that Karma is gone, I know Macy is going to be job hunting. I'd like to be the first one to offer her something that would be more of a challenge," I mused.

I'd been thinking about what a great addition Macy would be to the new center ever since we'd met.

"So, would you consider that an issue that would make a personal relationship a no-go?" he asked.

"Probably not for me," I told Dylan. "I'm the boss, but it could feel odd to her."

"Take it one day at a time," he advised. "You don't know if she'll accept a job with you or if she'll want to date you, either."

"I suppose I am jumping the gun," I agreed, although I didn't want to admit either one of those scenarios could happen.

"How are things there in Palm Springs?" he queried.

"Hot," I said honestly. "It might be getting into fall, but we're still just short of breaking triple digits during the hottest part of the day. It's nice in the evening and morning."

"It is a low desert climate," Dylan reminded me with a chuckle. "How are you liking the new house?"

"Love it," I answered. "It's nothing like those marvels of engineering that you and Damian have in London, but it's comfortable and it has spectacular views."

"I can't believe you've never bought a place in England but you had a home built for yourself in the States."

"This is going to be home base for the next year or two," I explained. "I figured I might as well be comfortable."

"I can't wait to get back to the US so Kylie and I can come see the new conservation center. I'm really proud of you, Leo," he said sincerely. "All joking aside about your love life, it takes an enormous amount of work to accomplish what you have so far at such a young age."

I knew he meant every word he said. I could hear the genuine pride in his tone. "Thanks. I'm doing what I love so it's easy to be devoted to it." I hesitated for a moment before I added earnestly, "It's good to have you back again, Dylan. Damian and I missed you more than you'll even know."

"Luckily, I'm not planning on falling off the deep end ever again, little brother," he said hoarsely. "I'll always be around when and if you need me. I've got way too much to be grateful for and to live for to go anywhere ever again."

"I'm glad you and Kylie worked everything out," I told him.

"It couldn't happen any other way," he rumbled. "There isn't another woman out there for me on the entire planet. I'm one lucky bastard."

Never in my wildest dreams could I have imagined hearing my brother talk about a woman like this, but I was ecstatic that he was doing it now.

"I think she'll be able to keep you in line," I joked.

"She's more than capable," he shot back with a laugh, not the least bit embarrassed to admit that he'd met his match. "Speaking of Kylie, I'd better get moving. She was putting something together for dinner."

I moved into the kitchen to pick up my wallet and sunglasses from the counter. "I'm headed to the center. Have a good dinner."

"Leo?" Dylan inquired.

"Yeah?"

He cleared his throat. "Maybe you should think about taking a little time off, too. Sometimes, if you're working all the time, you never look up and take the time to see what you're missing."

I thought about his words for a moment before I answered, "You might be right."

The two of us ended our call, but I thought about what he'd said for a long time after the conversation had concluded.

CHAPTER 6

Macy

"I WISH YOU WOULD have called me. I had no idea that you left London early with Leo," Kylie said remorsefully as we chatted on the phone.

I'd woken up late with a minor headache from my overindulgence in cocktails the night before. Other than that, there hadn't been any additional signs that I was suffering from a hangover.

One of the first things I'd done later this afternoon was to call Kylie and let her know what had happened since I hadn't seen her at the reception before I'd left England with Leo.

She'd caught me up on what had been happening with her for the last few days, and I'd been ecstatic when she'd told me that she and Dylan were now engaged.

"Everything happened so fast," I told her as I shifted positions on my couch to get more comfortable. "Leo was there offering to take me to the US immediately. I couldn't pass that offer up. It was too important for me to be there with Karma at the end. Really, he's been so amazing over the last few days."

"I feel horrible that I wasn't there," Kylie said sadly. "God Macy, I know how hard this must be for you."

"I'm doing okay," I told her honestly. "I think I did a lot of my mourning once I knew she wasn't going to survive the cancer and I've sobbed all over poor Leo for the last few days now. It's going to take a while for the pain of missing her to subside, but I'll just have to stay busy."

"You said you're taking the rest of this week off. What are your plans?" Kylie asked.

"I'll probably do some work at the shelter," I mused. "And Leo invited me out to Palm Springs to check out his progress on the new conservation center. Although I'm sure he was just trying to be nice because I was a basket case."

"I doubt that," Kylie pondered. "I mean, I don't know him all that well, but I think he takes his work pretty seriously. I doubt he would have asked you to visit if he didn't want to see you again. Honestly, you and Leo have so much in common. You should give the guy a shot."

I snorted. "You can't possibly be serious. Me…and Leo Lancaster?"

"Why not? You said you found him attractive when we were in London," Kylie argued. "Need I remind you that I just got engaged to a Lancaster?"

I sighed. "It's not just the billionaire thing or the aristocratic English family thing, although just those two things alone would be intimidating," I explained. "Leo Lancaster is considered a groundbreaking hero in the world of wildlife. I've watched everything that has ever been filmed about his field work. Add on the fact that he's utterly gorgeous and all of those things put him way out of my league."

"No, they do not," Kylie said insistently. "Leo is also human and you're not only gorgeous but incredibly successful yourself. I have no doubt he's attracted to you."

"He's not," I assured her. "And while I appreciate the fact that you think I'm attractive, I'm actually a woman who spends much of her time outside with no makeup and plenty of bad hair days. Not to mention the fact that I take care of large, wild creatures and end up smelling like them by the end of the day, too. Leo was simply being empathetic. He treats me like the little sister he never had."

"That makes sense because you're grieving and upset over Karma. He's definitely intelligent enough to know that hitting on you when you were so distressed wouldn't be a wise move."

I let out a quiet laugh. "God, I love you for thinking Leo Lancaster could actually be attracted to me. Kylie, you know me. I'm not a woman who worries about my appearance or who is afraid of getting my hands dirty. Never have been."

I was a jeans and T-shirt kind of woman who rarely left my hair out of my signature ponytail when I was working.

When I wasn't working, nothing changed much.

Most of my preferred outdoor activities weren't compatible with fancy clothing, dagger length nails or a ton of makeup.

"You've never needed the makeup or fancy clothes to look gorgeous," Kylie shot back. "I guarantee that Leo finds you attractive and I doubt he would have spent two days straight with you just to be nice. He's way too busy for that. Nor would he have invited you to Palm Springs before the center is even close to finished unless he wanted to see you again. I think you should take him up on his offer. Maybe it's time for *you* to have your fling with a Lancaster."

I knew Kylie was kidding me about having a fling with Leo because I'd challenged her to do the same with Dylan not long ago. "I'm pretty sure he needs to be attracted to me before I can have that little fling," I shot back at her.

Kylie let out an exasperated sigh. "I'm sure the attraction goes both ways."

"Think whatever you like," I told her amiably. "But you already know I'm socially awkward, especially with men."

"Did things feel awkward with Leo?" Kylie asked.

"Well, no. Not really. Although I'm sure that's because I was constantly crying on his shoulder over Karma. I wasn't thinking about anything else but her," I explained.

Strangely, things *hadn't* really been uncomfortable with Leo, even though I usually struggled to communicate with men on a date. Which was why I hadn't had one in a very long time.

For some reason, I was perfectly comfortable speaking about whatever was on my mind with Leo Lancaster.

"The circumstances should have made it even more awkward," Kylie observed. "Instead, you were comfortable enough to cry on his shoulder."

"I'm sure if I see him again under normal circumstances I'll go back to feeling like a bumbling idiot again. He's a pretty intimidating guy," I told her.

"His *resume* and his *money* might be intimidating, but *he* isn't," Kylie said. "Leo has always been so sweet to me."

"You're right," I conceded. "I don't think he has a snobby bone in his body."

Kylie hesitated for a moment before she asked, "I don't suppose you were comfortable enough with him to tell him about—"

"No, I didn't," I interrupted, already aware of what she wanted to know. "Jesus, Kylie. Do you really think I'd share things like that with a stranger?"

She sighed. "So what will you say if he starts asking questions about your life?"

"We don't know each other well enough for that," I assured her uncomfortably.

I wasn't ready to discuss the darkest part of my life with anyone except my closest friends.

Truthfully, I hadn't talked about it much at all, even to Kylie and Nicole.

Even after five years, it was easier to survive that way.

"I understand," Kylie said softly. "But I still think you should take some time off and try to do something other than work or volunteer. Going to Palm Springs would be a good change of scenery for you, Macy. Leo would be good company. You're physically and emotionally exhausted. I think you have been for a while now, and I know damn well that losing Karma has pushed you close to your limit."

She was right.

I wasn't even going to try to argue.

Both Kylie and Nicole knew me too well.

I'd used my arduous and intense residency to exhaust myself first.

Once that was over, I'd jumped into my work at the sanctuary, my adoration for Karma, and my volunteering projects to escape after my residency had ended.

Weariness and a distracted brain had been the only thing holding me together for the last five years and I was afraid to find out what would happen if I wasn't constantly working.

With Karma gone now and Kylie and Nicole so far away and unavailable to hang out with, I had no idea what I was going to do.

I massaged my temple to ease my lingering headache as I answered, "I am tired," I confessed. "I feel like it's been a chronic condition for me for a long time."

"Because you've never stopped long enough to rest," Kylie chastised gently.

My eyes filled with tears, but I blinked them back as I said shakily, "You know why I don't."

"I do. God, I really do understand, Macy. But I also love you like a sister and I'm worried about you."

I swallowed hard. "I'm fine, Kylie. It's been five years. Maybe I do need a break, but please don't worry about me. You and Nicole got me through the worst years."

"You've barely talked about it," Kylie said gently.

"Because I…can't." I explained. "But just having you two as my best friends helped me a lot."

And it had helped. Significantly. The love between Nicole, Kylie and I was sisterly and had always made me feel like I wasn't completely alone.

"Promise you'll take some time off just to relax," she pleaded. "No long days volunteering and no work. Maybe you could just spend some time with Hunter."

I smiled. "He definitely makes me laugh," I assured her. "Enough about me. Tell me about Dylan and the wedding. Any plans yet?"

I really wanted to change the subject, and I was relieved when I heard Kylie let out a sigh of capitulation before she said, "No plans yet. I'm still having a hard time believing he's in love with me, even though I'm wearing this big, gorgeous, flashy ring on my finger."

"I want a picture," I insisted. "You had no idea he was planning on proposing?"

"None," she said flatly. "In fact, I nearly screwed everything up. The man laid his heart at my feet and I crushed it before I realized he'd never actually done a single thing to hurt me. I'm glad he forgave me so easily. I nearly pushed away the best thing that had ever happened to me."

"Why?" I asked curiously.

She snorted. "Fear. My lack of belief that he was actually as crazy about me as I was about him. I messed up big time, Macy, and the crazy man still came after me."

"No offense," I said. "But I don't know why you couldn't see that. The rest of us all did. Dylan looked at you like a man who was completely devoted."

"I never saw it," she said in an awestruck tone. "I think I was way too wrapped up in my own concerns about how much I loved him. I was terrified he'd never love me back."

"And those fears were all for nothing," I teased. "I really wanted to hate Dylan after everything he'd done to Damian and Nicole, but I couldn't. He can be very charming, and he's so obviously crazy about you."

"I wanted to hate him, too," she agreed. "But I couldn't. He was in too much pain, and he'd punished himself enough."

I sighed. "I'm so glad you finally found the guy who's going to appreciate you and spoil you for the rest of your life. You deserve it."

Kylie's life hadn't been easy, especially when it came to relationships, so I was ecstatic that she'd finally found the right guy.

Early on, I'd had my concerns about Dylan Lancaster, but they turned out to be unfounded.

"You do realize that Nicole and I are going to be looking for your perfect guy now," she warned me. "We're way too happy not to want the same for you."

"Oh, God no," I told her empathically. "I'm perfectly content with my single status and my vibrator when it's convenient. The last thing I need is the hassle of a serious relationship. That long-term stuff has never gone well for me."

"Because you've never found the right guy," Kylie insisted. "And let's face it, you've never really had the time or energy to put into a long-term relationship before."

"It wasn't just that, and you know it. I always attracted the creepers or the losers. Even in high school. Very few guys are interested in wildlife nerds."

I hadn't had a boyfriend since I was an undergrad in college. None of the guys I'd dated after that had lasted long enough to be considered a serious relationship.

Then, five years ago, I'd decided I would never want another serious relationship in my life that required a deep emotional commitment.

I couldn't handle it.

Okay, maybe I wouldn't mind casual dating or possibly even a friends with benefits thing, even though I'd never tried that before.

I was tired of being lonely, but I wasn't equipped to handle the kind of relationships that Nicole and Kylie had with Damian and Dylan, either.

"None of those guys were good enough for you," Kylie said dismissively. "You don't need someone you have to take care of for God's sake. You had enough of those guys in your earlier dating years. You need someone who is as successful as you are and who adores your intelligence, so it would help if he's ridiculously smart, too. Oh, and he must love animals. No jerks who don't understand your love of wild creatures or your compassionate heart."

I smirked as I said, "Any other qualities this paragon needs to possess?"

I heard Kylie draw in a breath. "Yes, as a matter of fact, there are plenty more. He needs to put your needs before his, or at least make them just as important. It would also be nice if he's openly affectionate and attractive enough to make you forget all about your vibrator."

I laughed out loud. "I don't think a guy like that exists. At least, he hasn't trekked through my world."

"Then I guess we need to expand your world a little," Kylie shot back. "Seriously, Macy, do you really think that Nicole and I can be this happy and not try to find your Mr. Right for you?"

"I know you want me to be happy," I said lightly. "But not every woman dreams of finding the perfect guy to marry. I'm that female who would rather share my house with a dog or some other four legged animal, remember?"

"You dated way too many idiots," Kylie commented. "Not that I have room to criticize because most of my boyfriends were morons, too. Well, before Dylan that is. But there's a guy out there for you somewhere, Macy. A dog can't be there for you when you really need to talk."

What Kylie didn't realize was that I rarely wanted to talk about myself.

"Give it a rest, will you," I pleaded with Kylie, only partially joking. "You just got engaged. You can't start harping on me this hard already."

She laughed and finally dropped the subject.

We talked for another ten minutes before we finally hung up.

As soon as I'd hit the *Off* button, I stared at my cell for a moment, bringing up Leo's information as I did.

He'd made damn sure that we both added each other to our contacts on our cell phones before we'd left the bar the night before.

My thumb hovered over his number for a moment before I let out a pent-up breath and dropped the phone onto the side table.

"He's Leo-freaking-Lancaster, Macy," I chastised myself. "It's not like he's actually waiting for your call."

More than likely, he was hoping I didn't call because I'd already taken up so much of his time.

A tear trickled down my cheek as I thought about how good he'd been to me over the last few days.

He'd insisted that he wanted me to call him, but what else could he really say when I was a woman who was really connected to his new sister-in-law and to Dylan's fiancée as well?

It made sense that he was just being nice. He had an amazing mother who had obviously brought all of her sons up to be polite and kind.

Leo had gotten me through the hard part of Karma's passing.

The least I could do for him was to figure everything else out by myself instead of bumming him out, too.

CHAPTER 7

Leo

I GLANCED AT MY watch for the third time in ten minutes, and then cursed myself for giving into that compulsive instinct.

I was acting like a total idiot just because I was expecting Macy to arrive at any time now.

I'd given her an entire day to call me after I'd left her apartment.

When she hadn't given me a call by eight o'clock the following evening, I'd picked up my mobile and dialed her number.

Bloody hell! I'd wanted to see her again and I hadn't seen any point in wasting more time waiting for her to call me.

Once I'd gotten her on the phone, it had taken me fifteen minutes to convince her that I really *did* want her to come to Palm Springs, and then another thirty to talk her into bringing a suitcase so she could stay for the weekend.

The drive here and back to Newport Beach was just too much.

I'd convinced her that doing both drives in one day didn't leave us much time to check out the area.

She'd finally agreed to arrive today, which was Friday, and stay until Sunday.

Her concession had been somewhat weak and uncertain, but she hadn't changed her mind about coming. Thank fuck!

I looked around the living room as I drank a mug of tea, wondering what Macy would think of my house.

My place was a new contemporary that had some midcentury modern influences. The floor plan was extremely open, and everything was sprawled out on one level. Once someone entered through the front door, they could pretty much see all of the kitchen and the enormous living area.

My favorite part of the home was the floor to ceiling windows on two walls with expansive views of the desert and the pool and patio area off to one side.

I also had a few acres of property, which meant I didn't have neighbors right on top of me, which had been the best selling point to me.

Macy should be arriving any time now.

With Hunter in tow.

I grinned as I remembered that Macy had tried to tell me that she couldn't come because she needed to spend some time with Hunter because she'd been away.

She'd mumbled something about a wild cat that she'd recently adopted.

I'd told her to bring Hunter along.

Honestly, I was grateful for this new wild cat of hers because I knew that Macy would have otherwise insisted she stay in a hotel.

It wasn't as though I didn't like animals myself. I just traveled too damn much to have a pet.

The doorbell rang, and I was on my feet instantly and striding toward the door.

You're completely pathetic, Lancaster.

Even though I berated myself for jumping the second she arrived, it didn't slow me down.

I yanked the door open, and then stopped and gaped at the sight of Macy standing casually on my doormat.

Fuck! She was even more attractive than I remembered dressed in a pair of denim shorts and a pastel blue T-shirt with a touristy Hollywood logo on the front.

She was wearing almost no makeup and her hair was pulled back into some kind of clip, but she was still the most gorgeous female I'd ever laid eyes on.

I forced my gaze away from her and noticed that there was a rather large animal crate at her side.

"Hi," she said quietly. She'd shoved her sunglasses onto the top of her head and was staring up at me with those massive, serious gray eyes of hers. "You did say I could bring Hunter."

She looked uncomfortable, so I opened the door wide to let her in before she decided to bolt.

She didn't move to come inside as she asked, "Are you sure you're okay with Hunter being here? This is a really beautiful house. I'm not saying he's going to tear it up, but he can be a little…rambunctious."

"He's fine," I told her hastily as I picked up the crate and carried it into the house.

I didn't really care what he did to my house. I was so glad to see Macy that the damn feline could swing from the rooftops and destroy every piece of furniture I had and I wouldn't give a shit.

Macy had no choice but to follow me inside and close the door.

She was silent for a moment before she said, "I'm not sure I even told you that Hunter was a F-2 Bengal cat. Someone dumped him at the shelter a year ago, probably because he was sterile, which most of the males are for the first three generations of creating the hybrid. I took turns with the other vets there trying to socialize him and make sure he was trained. In the end, I took him permanently because I didn't have any other pets, and I adore him."

I put the crate down in the living room and crouched down to open it.

I finally understood that when Macy had said she had a *wild cat*, she'd meant that she *literally* had *a wild cat.*

Hunter strode out of his confinement looking slightly confused.

He was somewhat larger than an average domestic cat, and his brown, black and tan coat with rosette markings was incredibly striking.

I stayed crouched on Hunter's level so he didn't feel threatened, and waited to see if he'd approach me or ignore me.

"So he's a quarter Asian leopard cat?" I asked Macy quietly.

A leopard cat was a smaller wild cat native to the continental south, southeast, and East Asia.

The Asian leopard cat was slightly larger than a domestic cat, which obviously accounted for Hunter's larger body.

"Yes," she said, sounding impressed that I understood what the F-2 designation meant. "I'll never understand why people feel the need to breed wild cats with domestic felines when we have so many cats that need adopting. But Hunter is a handsome boy."

I grinned as Hunter headbutted me, and I reached out and petted the partially wild cat. "He doesn't seem to have a feral personality."

I knew that it took several generations to breed out all of the wild instincts of the crossbred cats sometimes.

She shrugged. "He doesn't. I mean, he's wicked smart, and he has quirks that domestic cats don't, but we worked on training him from the moment he came into the shelter. Sometimes he acts more like a dog than a cat. He'll play fetch with his cat toys, and he likes to go out for walks on a harness. He's a little odd at times, but not really wild."

"I'm more than happy to have him as a guest," I told her as Hunter flopped down at my feet so I could continue to worship him.

"I should run out and get his litter and his litter box," she said, sounding slightly anxious. "He's an indoor only cat."

I shook my head as I got to my feet. "Give me your keys and I'll get it. I'll bring your suitcase in, too. Anything else you need?"

"There's a few more things for Hunter in the passenger seat. His toys and a cooler with some food."

"Does he have to do a raw diet?" I asked curiously.

"No. Not really," she answered. "He gets a special food and I usually add some partially cooked chicken for him. Plus his vitamins."

As I walked out to her compact vehicle I had to admit that I admired the fact that she'd taken on a sterile cat that no one else had wanted.

Early generation wild cat hybrids could be a pain in the ass and usually required extra work to care for them properly.

Because the feline had so much wild cat blood, his nutritional needs were somewhat different.

As I came back through the door with the items I'd gone to retrieve, I heard Macy talking to Hunter.

"Shit! Come down from there, Hunter. God, I just told Leo that you aren't a crazy cat," she said in a nervous tone. "That's not *your* tree. We're guests here. You can't stay up there. Please."

I grinned as I noticed that Hunter had taken up residence in my ten foot Ficus tree in the corner. "He's fine," I told her as I set the items down on the floor. "They spend part of their lives living in the trees in the wild. He'll come down when he feels more comfortable."

Macy turned to me with a pensive expression. "It's a silk tree. I'm sure it was custom made, Leo. He'll probably tear it apart with his claws."

I shrugged. "It's replaceable. He's obviously more at ease there for now. Leave him, Macy. It's no big deal. Can I get you something to drink?"

I watched as she looked from me to the tree, and then let out a huge sigh. "Don't say that I didn't warn you. I'd love some water. It's pretty hot out there already, and it's not even noon yet."

"It's going to be in the high nineties today," I told her. "But it's supposed to be cooler tomorrow and Sunday."

I walked into the kitchen as she wandered over to the windows. "Your views are amazing, Leo. There's something incredibly powerful about the desert."

"It's strange that you feel that way," I replied as I handed her the glass of ice water. "I feel the same, but some people think the desert is stark and lifeless."

She shook her head. "It's never lifeless and I think it's so fascinating because it can be so dangerous. It's probably like looking at a tornado. You want to look away, but you're mesmerized by it."

I motioned for her to have a seat on the sofa. Once she was seated, I sat at the other end as I said, "Are you doing okay? You seem a little nervous."

Maybe we'd only spent two days together, but it was an intense and personal few days.

I'd been the guy who had held her in my arms while she cried on my shoulder.

I'd been the guy who had gotten her thoroughly pissed and then helped her get back home.

I'd been the guy she'd talked to about how painful Karma's death had been.

I *wasn't* the guy she needed to be uncomfortable with at this point.

She swallowed a mouthful of water before she answered, "Maybe I'm still not quite convinced that you're thrilled to have me here. I keep wondering whether you offered just to be polite."

I raised a brow. How in the hell could she still think *that*? "I called you, remember?"

She gave me that solemn, gray-eyed stare that always made me want to make her smile as she replied, "I know. And I'm still trying to figure out why."

"Is it really so hard for you to believe that I just want to spend time with you, Macy? That I like you and wanted to see you again?"

She nodded slowly. "Yeah, really hard to believe, actually. I haven't exactly been good company for you so far, and what woman brings her wild cat on a date? Okay, wait, not that we're actually dating—"

"I consider this a date," I told her bluntly as I moved closer to her. "And you could have brought an entire zoo if that's what it took for me to see you again. I like you, Macy. I want to spend more time with you and get to know you. I think you already know that I'm attracted to you."

Her eyes grew wide. "Why? I'm not your type. At all."

"What exactly is my type?" I asked huskily as I reached out and tucked an errant lock of hair behind her ear.

She put her water down on the coffee table as she answered, "I don't know. Some supermodel or a woman who grew up in your aristocratic circle. Not some female who spends all of her time with animals and hardly knows how to make conversation with an attractive guy like you."

"You seem to be doing just fine," I assured her. "Can you honestly say you can't feel the same chemistry between us that I do?"

Impossible.

That magnetic pull was there between us, and there was no way she wasn't feeling the same thing.

Maybe I'd thought she wasn't interested before, but the strange energy was even more powerful today.

She shook her head. "I thought it was just me."

Because I didn't want to freak her out by moving too fast, I simply slipped my arm around her shoulders and rested my forehead against hers as I said, "You've gotten my dick hard since the first time I met you. Apparently, supermodels and uptight women don't do a thing for me."

I could feel her warm breath on my face as she said, "Prove it. If you're so attracted to me, then kiss me, Leo. Let's see what kind of chemistry we have."

Bloody hell! If she thought she was going to have to ask me twice, she was wrong.

There was no possible way I could ignore that challenge.

I took her face in my hands and lowered my mouth to hers before she had a chance to change her mind.

CHAPTER 8

Macy

I LET OUT A small moan as Leo's mouth covered mine, still wondering why in the hell I'd asked him to kiss me.

Maybe I'd been just as curious as he was to figure out why I was so damn drawn to him.

Maybe I wanted to know if he really felt the same thing I did.

Maybe…I'd just been dying for him to kiss me.

It definitely wasn't something I'd normally say to a guy. Then again, Leo Lancaster was no ordinary man.

He's right. There's definitely some crazy chemistry between the two of us today. It's not my imagination.

Leo Lancaster wanted me, and he was making damn sure I knew it, even though he wasn't touching anything except for my face.

Every nerve ending in my body sizzled as he nibbled on my bottom lip, insisting that I open for him, which I did almost immediately.

His masculine scent invaded my senses and fierce desire like I'd never experienced before flooded my entire being.

Okay. Yeah. Maybe I'd had a mad crush on him when he'd been just an attractive, brilliant guy on my television screen.

But it hadn't felt like this.

Nothing had ever felt like this.

I wrapped my arms around his neck and buried my fingers into the hair at his nape.

He felt so damn good, smelled so damn good, that I couldn't stop myself from touching him.

It had been so long since I'd felt like an attractive woman that I was reveling in the knowledge that Leo really did want me.

I was drowning in his desire as it mingled with my own.

"Leo," I said breathlessly as he finally released my lips.

"Christ! I'm sorry, Macy," he said in a frustrated voice as he backed away from me. "I've wanted to kiss you since the day we met, and I got a little carried away." He ran a hand through his hair as he added, "I hope you're convinced now. If not, I'm going to want to try again."

I smiled as I said softly, "Then maybe I should pretend like I'm not persuaded."

He grinned back at me, looking relieved as he answered, "I'd have no problem working harder at converting you to the truth." In a more earnest voice, he added, "I don't know why you even thought there was nothing there when the attraction so obviously exists."

"It's been a long time for me, Leo," I told him honestly, seeing no reason not to be sincere after everything he'd done for me. "And I'm not sure I've ever been this attracted to someone. But you're Leo Lancaster for God's sake. There's probably a gazillion women that would love to sleep with you."

He pulled me closer as he replied, "It's been a while for me, too, and I guarantee I've never been this attracted to anyone, either. I don't sleep with every woman I meet, Macy, and most of the time I'm out in the field where my last thought is about getting laid. Believe it or not, I've never been quite as smooth with women as Dylan and Damian. I'm usually the guy who gets put firmly in the friend zone because I have an odd preoccupation about being outside and getting dirty instead of preferring to spend my time like other rich men do."

Holy shit! What in the hell was wrong with the women he'd dated or been interested in? "They're crazy," I told him. "I've seen your documentaries. There's something incredibly hot about you when you decide to get...dirty. And you seemed at home with all of the social events for the wedding."

He grinned. "There's a difference between going through the motions and enjoying them. Granted, I wasn't faking the fact that I was thrilled to be at my brother's wedding, but for the most part, I usually hate the stuffy affairs. I was raised to be part of that world, but most of the time I'm counting the hours until I can escape from that particular crowd."

I leaned back and rested my body against his solid form, no longer feeling awkward about touching him. "So was it weird not wanting the same thing that your older brothers did when you were younger?"

Leo started to toy with a lock of my hair as he answered thoughtfully, "Honestly, not really. I had amazing parents, and neither one of them ever made me feel different because my interests weren't the same as Dylan's and Damian's. My father saw their interest in Lancaster International so he groomed them to take over someday. He took the same interest in advancing my education about wildlife when he saw that my interests were in that field. He never made me feel different or less than because I didn't want to take over Lancaster International with Damian and Dylan. Both he and Mum were proud of me no matter what kind of career I chose."

"I didn't get to know Bella all that well because she was so busy with the wedding, but I could see that kindness in your mom, and I know how good she's been to Nicole," I told Leo. "She's an incredible woman."

"She is," he acknowledged. "My father was just as extraordinary."

My hand instinctively went to cover his. I knew that Leo had lost his father several years ago. "You must miss him."

"Every day," he said huskily. "They say it gets easier, and maybe it does, but I still miss him nearly as much as I did the day he died. The pain of the loss just gets less acute over time."

"You're right. It gets easier, but that soul deep ache of missing someone never really goes away," I told him without thinking about my response.

He tightened his arm around me protectively. "So you've already lost your father, too?" he asked.

My heart stuttered.

It wasn't like I hadn't known the subject would come up.

I'd just hoped it wouldn't be this soon.

For some reason, I couldn't just blow off Leo's question.

He'd done too much for me, seen too much of me emotionally for me not to tell him the truth.

I nodded. "Yes."

Granted, this was something I didn't like to talk about, but if Leo and I were going to spend time together he'd find out about it eventually.

"Where is your mum?" he questioned gently.

"Also dead," I said flatly.

"Siblings?" he queried once more.

"One brother," I said as tears welled up in my eyes. "He's gone, too. Five years ago, I lost all three of them in an instant during my residency in San Diego. My younger brother Brandon was home from the university on a holiday break. He was just about to finish his master's degree in aerospace engineering, and my parents wanted to celebrate by taking a trip with him to Catalina Island by helicopter. People do it every day and nothing has ever happened. It's just a short hop as far as flights go. It's usually extremely safe, but something unusual happened that day. The helicopter went down over the Pacific Ocean from engine failure. My father, mother, brother and the pilot all died. Their bodies were recovered the next day."

Leo was silent for a moment before he cursed, "Fuck! You lost your entire family in one incident?"

"Yes. One day they were all there and we were a happy family, and the next day I was completely alone trying to figure out how to bury all of them," I said in a tremulous voice.

It had been so long since I'd talked about my family that something broke wide open inside me now that I was sharing that tragedy with someone else.

"Christ, Macy," he said hoarsely as he wrapped his other arm around me like he could somehow protect me. "I'm so bloody sorry. How do you live through something like that? I lost my father and I felt like I wasn't going to make it through that pain. But that was nothing compared to losing your whole family."

Tears started to freely flow down my cheeks. Now that I'd started, I wasn't going to stop until everything was out there. "There were days when I wasn't sure I'd make it, and then there were days that I was numb because I couldn't handle the pain anymore. It was hard, Leo. It still is. We were really close. Once I got everything settled in Newport Beach, I wasn't sure if I could go back to my residency in San Diego, but I knew I had to do it. Mom and Dad helped me with my education, and they'd want me to keep going. They worked hard to help Brandon and I with college so neither of us graduated with an overwhelming amount of student debt. Dad had his own small plumbing service and Mom was a librarian, so they weren't exactly loaded. I pushed myself to leave Newport

Beach and go back to San Diego. I knew my parents would be disappointed if I didn't, but I was still in so much shock that I felt like I was just going through the motions for a while. Spending time with Karma, Nicole and Kylie were about the only things that kept me sane. Unfortunately, Nic wasn't living here in California when it happened and Kylie had her own challenges back then, so my main confidante was usually Karma."

"So losing her reminded you of that pain all over again?" Leo asked gently.

I nodded. "I poured my heart out to her when I needed some kind of comfort. Maybe it's crazy, but sometimes I think she understood because she'd been through so much pain herself."

"It's not crazy. She helped you cope. How do you deal with the stress of a demanding residency and get through the pain of losing your whole family?" Leo asked hoarsely.

I closed my eyes and my entire body shuddered as I remembered how difficult it had been back then. "I'm not sure I completely dealt with the pain. I had to stifle most of it," I explained. "I escaped into the difficulty of my residency, tried to fill every single moment of my day so I could stay in denial. That worked for a while, but day after day of not talking to my family nearly broke me. My parents and I were in contact all the time and Brandon and I were best friends. He was my little brother. If we didn't talk, we at least texted every day. It's been five years, but there are still moments when I panic because I suddenly realize that I've gone from being part of a happy family to being completely alone."

He ran his hands up and down my arms in a soothing motion. "I don't know how in the fuck you managed," he rasped close to my ear. "The loss of one parent is soul crushing. I don't know how you deal with losing everyone."

I shrugged. "Sometimes life doesn't give us a choice of what we have to handle. That loss left its mark and I haven't been good at relationships since that day. Not that I was all that great with romantic relationships before that, but now I suck at dating, Leo. Maybe I don't want to care about anyone else because I know that nothing lasts forever. Happiness is fleeting. One day you're flying high and the next day fate takes away everything and everyone you love."

"That's not completely true, Macy. Happiness can last, and you can fly high for a long time without crashing," Leo said in a low, patient tone. "But I know why you feel the way you do."

Emotions I hadn't dealt with in years rose up inside me and I choked back a sob.

Leo lifted me into his lap and supported my body while I rested my head against his shoulder and let loose the kind of sorrow that eats a person's soul.

He didn't speak.

He didn't try to fix anything.

Leo simply held me like he'd never let go while I wailed and soaked his T-shirt with my tears.

"God, I-I'm so s-sorry," I stuttered as the sobs subsided. "I've lost count of how many times I've done this to you in the last few days."

Leo stroked a gentle hand over the back of my head as he put his mouth close to my ear and said, "I'm here for you anytime you need to cry. You've been so incredibly strong, Macy, but you don't have to be alone anymore."

I drew back and started to swipe the tears from my eyes.

I wasn't sure how it had happened, but Leo Lancaster had actually become a safe place to fall for me. Probably because he would never be the type to judge or try to brush off anyone's sorrow.

"I don't talk about my family much," I told him. "It's too difficult to talk about, but I wanted you to know because you've been so amazing over the last several days. God, things are never emotional like this for me. I know it's probably difficult for you to understand the connection between Karma and my family—"

"It's not," he said decisively. "She was your confidante and your consoler when you were alone and confused out of your mind."

I nodded. "Most people would think I'm crazy."

"Most people forget humans are animals. We're supposed to be the most intelligent of them all. I have my doubts about that sometimes," he grumbled drily.

I laughed and then tensed when I heard what sounded like a toilet flushing down the main hallway of Leo's gorgeous home.

"What the hell?" Leo said as his arms tightened around me. "I'd swear that was *my* toilet, but nobody else is here."

My eyes shot to the tree where Hunter had been, and then down the main hallway as the toilet flushed again…and again.

Yep. That's what I thought.

"Ummm…do you remember when I told you that Hunter had a few weird quirks?" I asked Leo, my tone filled with trepidation. "Probably the first thing I should have warned you about was his affinity for water. Any water. I mean, he really, really loves water of any kind. In fact, he loves it so much that he'll flush the toilet over and over again just to watch and feel it swirl if you don't close toilet lids."

I turned my head to look at his face as he processed what I'd just said.

At first, he looked disbelieving.

As the toilet flushed again, he appeared to be somewhat startled.

Then when it happened one more time, I could tell he was finally a believer.

Leo Lancaster grinned, threw his head back and let out the most gloriously amused laugh I'd ever heard.

CHAPTER 9

Leo

"THIS IS AMAZING, Leo. All of it. It's the perfect place for a conservation center and this rehab area is huge," Macy said with a huge sigh as she looked around the inside of the rehab center on Saturday.

I watched as she surveyed the large indoor facility.

She was dressed casually in a pair of jeans, sandals and a white T-shirt with a San Diego Zoo logo and pictures of birds and a large koala on the front.

I smirked because she obviously collected T-shirts from the places she'd worked or visited, just like I did.

I'd opted to pull on a well-worn Chester Zoo T-shirt this morning and a pair of jeans, my standard dress whenever I was headed for the conservation center.

My eyes roamed over the rounded curves of Macy's ass when she bent over to look at some of our equipment.

Christ! The temptation was right there and it was really difficult to ignore a cock teasing sight like that.

"*Meep! Meep! Meep!*"

I scowled down at Hunter as he spoke to me in his feline language. He was obviously trying to tell me what a pervert I was, and he was right.

"What did you expect me to do, mate?" I asked as I picked up the cat and scratched behind his ears. "Ignore what was literally right in front of me?"

I almost felt guilty as Hunter shot me an intense green-eyed stare, as though he was trying to tell me that I shouldn't ogle Macy like a creeper.

"Not possible," I grumbled. "She's much too beautiful to ignore."

The cat continued to shoot me what I perceived to be an admonishing look and then butted his head against my shoulder before licking the side of my face.

During the last twenty-four hours, I'd learned how to co-exist with the water loving feline.

At first, I'd found his obsession with water somewhat amusing, but I'd quickly realized that it was going to be necessary to seriously Hunter-proof my home right after he'd gotten into the bathroom last night while I was showering. He'd easily found a way to get into the shower with me by entering at the top of the enclosure.

Not only had he scared the shit out of me, but I'd had to get him under control before he decided to use my balls as a chew toy and luxuriate in the warm water like it was there for *his* enjoyment.

Bloody hell! The cat was dangerously smart. Much smarter than any domestic cat I'd ever encountered.

He was currently touring the facility on a harness with Macy, and not only was he well-trained on that kitty leash, but he also followed commands for her.

The only time he got out of line was when he was tempted by water.

Even then, Hunter managed to look somewhat shamed after he was caught messing with water, but it didn't seem to totally discourage him from doing it again.

Problem was, he was also incredibly affectionate, so it was very difficult to get too upset with the monster.

Really, was it a big deal that I had to keep the toilet seat down when he was around because Hunter would do nothing to help the drought situation in California with his toilet flushing obsession?

Nope. It really wasn't. Nor was it that much of an imposition to make sure the bathroom door was closed and locked when I needed to shower.

Hunter I could handle.

However, I still wasn't quite sure what to make of Macy's revelations the day before.

What she'd experienced was unfathomable to me.

I'd lost my father, but I'd had my mother and my brothers to lean on when we were all grieving.

Who had Macy had?

I knew that Nicole and Kylie had been there for Macy, but they hadn't been very close geographically at the time.

She'd lost her entire family in one accident.

What in the fuck would it feel like to be part of a loving family one moment and completely alone the next?

I stroked my hand over Hunter's soft coat as I watched Macy stroll back toward the treatment rooms.

It would be bloody unbearable to go through what she had, yet here she was, still surviving and incredibly successful in her career.

There was no possible way that the experience hadn't left its share of damage, but just the fact that she'd stayed upright and functioning was a fucking miracle to me.

She'd managed to cope by throwing herself into helping animals and not completely dealing with the tragedy.

Maybe that had been the only way to grapple with her heartache because taking it in all at once would have likely crushed her until she couldn't function.

I wish I could have been there to protect her.

Like having me around would have kept her from feeling the desolation and anguish of losing her family?

No, she still would have been in an agonizing state of mourning, but at least someone would have been there to hold her, to remind her that not everyone she cared about in her life had left her.

"Meep!"

"Sorry, mate," I told Hunter as I realized I'd squeezed his body just a little too hard because I was thinking about Macy's horrific experience.

I put Hunter down on the ground and let him drag the leash around as he explored. We were indoors and since the rehab was empty, there was very little trouble the cat could get into at the moment.

"No doubt you'll have a variety of species to rehab," Macy said as she started to walk back toward me. "This area and Palm Springs sits so close to so many wildlife corridors and it's surrounded by the mountains. Bears, bobcats, mountain lions and other large prey animals are some possibilities."

I nodded. "There are a lot of endangered species in the Coachella Valley, too, from toads and frogs to Peninsular Bighorn sheep. Obviously, our goal will be to rehab and release as much as possible."

Macy smiled at me as she said, "This is one very ambitious project."

I shook my head. "Not nearly as ambitious as my facility in England. The biggest challenges will occur in the first year or so, when we're setting up habitats for our captive breeding. It's chaotic when you're establishing programs for more than one species at a time."

"I'm really excited that you're getting involved in trying to recover the numbers of critically endangered wolf species," Macy said enthusiastically. "Will all of your captive breeding be mammals?"

"Here, yes," I confirmed. "We won't be set up for anything else. The facility is too small, and we'll be partially focused on rehab, too. I won't take on more than we can do extremely well."

"Very wise," she said as she shot me an admiring look that made me feel like a fucking god.

Maybe our first few days together had been difficult, but I'd quickly discovered that being with Macy under normal circumstances was the best damn feeling in the world.

"I'm sorry it didn't cool off all that much for you today," I said as she picked up Hunter's leash.

She shot me a wicked grin as she straightened up. "I know a place that's a lot cooler," she said in a teasing voice.

I lifted a brow. "Tell me."

"It's usually a lot cooler when you're above eight thousand feet. Have you done the tram yet?" she asked.

Brilliant! I should have thought about that myself.

"Heard about it," I confessed. "But I haven't had a chance to take the ride up yet."

She wrinkled her nose adorably. "It's terribly touristy, but you really should go at least once."

"Have you been?" I asked curiously.

She nodded. "Several times, but I haven't been on it for years. The last time I rode on it I was here with my family."

Fuck! I hated even the small amount of melancholy that crept into her gaze. "Are you sure you want to do it? The last thing I want to do is bring up painful memories for you, Macy."

She shook her head. "They aren't sad memories, and maybe it's time I talked about them. They were happy times, and I've gone with friends, too. My dad used to love all the cheesy tourist stuff, and we adored him for it. We had so much fun chasing those tourist traps. I think Brandon and I held some kind of record for the kids who visited Disney and all of the other theme parks the most times as children."

I wrapped my arm around her waist as we walked out of the rehab center because I couldn't help myself. I wanted to be close to her in case I could help fill the emptiness she must feel at times.

It killed me to think about Macy being alone and hurting, but I knew that's exactly where she'd been many times over the last five years.

She'd talked about needing to be in denial to some extent.

She'd obviously needed to release a little of her sorrow over a long period of time so it didn't all explode at the same time, which would have been unbearable.

"How many times?" I asked since she seemed almost happy to relive some of the better times with her family now.

She shrugged. "I lost count after twenty-five, but we went a lot. So, if you're game to go on the tram, I'll make us lunch and we can explore when we get to the top. We'll have to stop at your house, and you'll have to lend me a sweatshirt. It's not like I anticipated needing anything warm."

I grinned as I watched her face. I could almost hear the wheels turning in her brain as she quickly planned the impromptu trip.

"I don't suppose we can take Hunter," I mused.

"He's not allowed on the tram. He'll have to stay behind on this trip. Be careful," she warned teasingly. "I'm going to start to think you like him, even though he almost nailed you in the balls."

I raised my brow. "Oh, so you think that's funny, do you?"

She released something that sounded suspiciously like a giggle. "Actually, I do. I can't help myself. That's something I never had to worry about the first time he snuck into my shower."

Bloody hell! Picturing what that shower would look like was the last thing I needed to be doing, but I wanted her curvy body wrapped around me naked so badly that I couldn't stop my brain from going there.

I pulled her to a stop, wrapped my other arm around her and pulled her to face me as we hit some shade under a tree. "I happen to be extremely fond of the family jewels, woman," I told her in a mock growl.

She glanced up at me with an innocent look on her face. "I'm sure you are. Unfortunately, it sounded like Hunter found them pretty fascinating, too."

"He's a menace," I pronounced jokingly.

"You like him," she accused.

"Guilty," I admitted as I moved closer and pinned her between my body and the tree trunk. "How can I not be fascinated by a cat that can play fetch, walk on a leash, and flush a toilet? You did a fantastic job of training him by the way."

She shrugged. "I wasn't responsible for the toilet trick. He figured that out on his own, and it wasn't just me. I had help."

I was beginning to realize that her response was typical Macy. She rarely took sole credit for anything she did or accomplished.

I rested a palm on the tree above her head and stared down into her beautiful eyes. The shadows were still there, but they were a lighter gray than they'd been when she'd been anticipating Karma's death.

She looked happier.

She looked more at ease.

She looked…like the sexiest woman I'd ever laid eyes on.

"I'm going to kiss you if you don't stop me," I warned her huskily.

She put a hand on my chest but she didn't push me away. "Leo, you already know that I don't do relationships well. Even before I lost my entire family, I was ridiculously awkward on dates. I haven't had a regular boyfriend since my undergrad years, and it's been almost that long since I've had sex. Nevertheless, I still want you to kiss me, and I'm not sure what to do about that."

My heart slammed against my chest wall as I saw the way she devoured me with her eyes.

She wanted.

She needed.

And fuck me! I wanted to give Macy Palmer everything she wanted and more.

"Did I ask you for anything?" I questioned.

She shook her head as she said, "No."

"Do you really think, after what you told me, that I'd start demanding anything from you?"

She swallowed hard. "Probably not."

"Then why in the hell are you so worried? I want to steal a kiss. That's it. For now," I said in a husky voice.

Alright, so maybe I wanted a hell of a lot more from her, but I wasn't a complete prick. I wasn't going to ask for more than she could give me right now.

She swiftly wrapped her arms around my neck and jerked my head down. "Okay," she said breathlessly. "Then steal all the kisses you want."

I grinned at her enthusiasm as I swooped in and stole her lips, and then plundered way longer than I should have.

She was so fucking sweet and the more I tasted, the more I wanted.

Macy Palmer made me feel things I hadn't felt since I was a teenager, and I wasn't sure I liked it.

I had almost zero control every damn time I touched her.

She released a small moan against my lips, and my cock was instantly rock-hard and ready to satisfy her.

Fuck!

I had to force myself to release her lips so she could take a breath, and I could pull my shit together.

It was pure hell letting her go because I knew she wanted me as much as I wanted her.

I held her until she stopped panting against my shoulder and then stepped back and freed her.

I dropped my forehead against her shoulder as I grumbled, "You'd better take me somewhere cooler after that, woman."

She laughed lightly, like a bloody seductress, and I instantly decided every moment of my current torture was absolutely worth it.

CHAPTER 10

Macy

"I'M GOING TO end up completely spoiled," Leo pronounced as he spread more feta dip on a pita chip. "This is the best lunch I've had in a long time."

My belly completely full, I stretched out on the large blanket we'd spread out off of the hiking trail near the peak of the San Jacinto Mountains.

We'd ridden the tram up and hiked for a while before we found a place to scarf down the lunch I'd hastily put together at Leo's house.

"Then you're obviously deprived," I said with a chuckle. "I didn't exactly have time to put together a gourmet lunch."

I knew from past experience that the snack bar and deli at the top of the mountain didn't have very appetizing food. I'd thrown something together at Leo's place after making a quick stop at the grocery store.

"Doesn't matter," he told me. "Nobody ever makes me lunch, and this is fantastic."

Nobody ever made him lunch? How is that possible? Didn't most billionaires have a chef of some kind?

I knew that Leo's mother had staff at her estate in England, but Leo apparently didn't spend much time there.

"Don't you have someone who cooks for you?" I asked.

He swallowed and took a slug of water before he answered, "Never. My schedule is unpredictable. I either throw something in the microwave or I just get takeaway."

I smiled at his usage of the British term for takeout. "I shoved some premade dough into the oven for cookies, stuffed some sandwich rolls with egg salad, and stirred up some feta dip, which took about five minutes. As an afterthought I added some fruit to make up for the cookies. It's not exactly gourmet food, Leo."

He shrugged. "It's special to me. Thank you for doing it, and for thinking about a way for us to cool off. It's incredible up here."

I sighed. God, he was so easy to please and so damn thoughtful. I couldn't think of a single guy in my past that would have thanked me for throwing together some food.

"My mom liked to cook and bake," I shared, surprised that I was feeling so comfortable about sharing some family things with Leo. "But she had a busy job, so she didn't always have time to spend in the kitchen. I learned a lot from her about getting a decent meal on the fly."

"And your father?" Leo questioned.

I smiled. "He liked to eat so he helped with dishes. We all did."

Leo started to put the food containers in the backpack he'd brought. "I'd definitely be on dish detail," he confessed. "I'm not good in a kitchen. The only thing I can manage to cook is British pancakes. And the only reason I can cook those is because my brothers and I made them with our parents. It was something we did as a family, but we otherwise had a cook who fed us on a daily basis. We were definitely privileged."

He sounded so guilty that I replied. "There's nothing wrong with that if you have the money to hire someone. Your father was a billionaire duke with an enormous corporation and your mother still seems like she has a million things to do every day for her charities. I'm sure time was money in your household and it was much easier just to have someone to do the little things that are so time consuming. I'm just surprised you don't have someone to cook for you now."

He zipped his backpack and picked up his water as he answered, "I've actually never had a personal home of my own. The one in Palm Springs is my first. My conservation center in England has an area with sleeping quarters since the staff has to occasionally stay if there's something critical happening. I stay there when I'm at the center. If I'm near the city, I'm there to see Mum, so I stay at the estate. Renting is an option if I need to stay somewhere for a while. More often than not, I'm traveling. I've just never seen the point in owning a place until now."

My eyes widened. "Why now?"

He grinned and my heart skittered at that devilish smile. "I'm all grown up," he answered. "I know my primary residence is going to be here for a while, and I'm starting to slow down on my travel. It would be nice to sleep in a real bed more often. I'll still send my team out for exploration, but I don't always have to be with them. This conservation center is important to me and I'd like to spend more time at the one in England as well. I have good staff, but there's only so much they can authorize in my absence. I've missed some opportunities to help by being out of contact so much."

I'd never really thought about how uncomfortable it had been for Leo to be sleeping out in the forest…or a jungle…or the mountains…or any place so remote that he might find extinct animals that still existed. Yeah, some of it might be exciting, but he'd already admitted that it was lonely.

"I liked to camp when I was younger," I confessed. "But I don't think it's something I'd want to do all the time."

He shrugged. "I guess I just got used to it because it goes with the job if I want to go where the endangered wildlife lives."

I shook my head as I looked at him. "You're so amazing, Leo."

And God, he really was incredible.

How many rich guys would give up a very cushy life to pursue their passion for wildlife?

I'd known plenty of male zoologists, wildlife biologists and exotic vets. I was willing to bet that very few of them were willing to deal with the uncomfortable conditions necessary to do what Leo had done for years.

He grinned. "I think you're the only one who thinks so. Everyone else thinks I'm batshit crazy."

I put my forefinger and my thumb close together as I said, "There might be just a tiny bit of crazy in there, too."

He shook his head. "Too late. You already professed that I was amazing. I'm keeping that opinion."

I laughed. I couldn't help myself. Leo was as amusing as he was gorgeous.

"Will you miss being out in the field all the time?" I questioned.

"Most of it, no," he told me. "The only thing I'll miss is finding some hope that we haven't managed to kill off a species completely. I'm sure there will be certain cases that I'll want to investigate personally, but the work I'm doing for conservation here and at the center in England is important, too. Nothing ends in the field when we find proof that a species exists. That's just the beginning. It carries on with the hard work that has to be done on a day-to-day basis to save that species."

He was right. Once a critically endangered species was recognized, there was a lot more to do than just to find them in the wild.

"I can't wait to see everything that happens here," I said excitedly. "It has to be gratifying to be involved in the captive breeding programs, too."

He shrugged. "When they work. You and I both know that sometimes there are more failures than successes when it comes to captive breeding. Especially when you want to reintroduce them into the wild. Sometimes it's exhilarating and sometimes it's soul killing."

I nodded. "I can only imagine. I assume it's the success stories that keep you going."

"Always," he said emphatically. "One success can make up for quite a few failures."

"I get it," I agreed. "One animal life saved for me is enough to prop me up after losing another one. We do what we can, right? And it makes a difference."

He swallowed a gulp of water before he said, "We wouldn't be doing it if we didn't think we were making a difference."

"I'm glad I'll be around to watch your center grow," I said honestly.

Leo's brow furrowed and he took a deep breath. "Macy, I really want to talk to you about the center here."

"Problems?" I asked, concerned.

"No. I don't want to talk to you about issues. I guess I've been trying, not very successfully, to feel you out about how you'd respond to a job offer. I'm going to need a veterinary medical director. You said you were going to be looking for a challenge. I'm wondering if that job might fit your criteria."

I gaped at Leo, momentarily stunned into silence.

There were only two Lancaster conservation centers in the entire world, and Leo Lancaster had just asked me if I'd be interested in being the medical director for one of them.

Completely.

Speechless.

It was the type of job that you hoped you were qualified for somewhere down the road—after a few decades into your career.

Yeah, I was an exotic vet. I had those qualifications.

Yeah, I'd had a really impressive residency for three years that had gotten me a ton of experience with all different types of wildlife.

However, any experience I'd gotten with the breeding programs at the zoo had been heavily supervised by a senior vet because I didn't have the experience behind me in captive breeding.

Yeah, I'd also been practicing for a few years in a very reputable big cat rescue.

But oh, holy shit, nothing could have prepared me for *this* job offer.

Working for Leo's prestigious, state-of-art conservation center would be *the* dream job for any zoological vet, and I knew there were exotic vets that were a lot more qualified than me.

"L-Leo," I stammered. "I don't even know what to say. God, I can't think of any exotic vet who would turn down your offer. Everything you do is on the cutting edge of technology and veterinary medicine. But I don't have the experience you need. I've never been heavily involved in a captive breeding program."

"That's exactly what my medical director, Jaya, said when I offered her the same job at the center in England. She was your age, Macy, with a similar background. She was one of the best decisions I ever made. Yes, there is some information about captive breeding that crosses all species, but for the most part, every time you get a new species to breed, you're learning all over again. Every single one is different. The breeding habits are different. When I take on a new species for captive breeding, that comes with experts who train my people about that particular breed until my staff is comfortable handling things without the experts around. I can bring Jaya over to help you until you feel more comfortable if you think that would help. I think she'd be happy to do it. Besides skill, the one thing that's essential for the job is passion. You have that. You'd be an incredible addition to the team here, and you'd be with me in every interview for your support staff. Once you're comfortable, I doubt you'll need my input."

"What about the rehab center?" I asked, still stunned.

"You'll oversee it since you'll be the medical director of the center, but we'll hire staff for the day-to-day running of the rehab. Most of your time and responsibilities will be dedicated to the animals in the captive breeding programs, and please know that you won't be doing it alone. It takes an entire team for each species."

My head was spinning by the time he stopped talking.

I wanted to scream with excitement and tell him that of course I'd take the job.

But…I hesitated.

I wanted to be sure I wasn't going to disappoint him.

"Could I have some time to think about it? And would you mind if I spoke with Jaya just to get some idea about her responsibilities?"

He nodded. "Of course. I'm not a vet, so I can't give you a vet's perspective about what the job is like."

I shot him a longing look. "Don't get me wrong, I want to accept, Leo. Hell, any vet would want to take this job. I just want to make sure I'm right for the position."

"If I didn't think you were, I wouldn't have offered it," Leo said in a solemn tone. "I won't lie to you and say that I'm not attracted to you, but that has nothing to do with this job offer. Take your time and make sure it's right for you. We have a month or two before you'll actually have to report to the center every day, but I'd need an answer before that so we can start working on hiring more staff. I know you'll have to give your notice to the sanctuary."

"I already did," I said softly. "I called the director and let him know I was leaving at the end of next week. He hired my replacement a few months ago after I told him I'd be leaving once Karma was gone. He's fine with it. He's prepared. He's known that I'd be leaving for months now and he understands how hard it would be for me to stay there now that Karma's gone. He knows I want to move on and use more of my skills somewhere else."

"You're going back to the sanctuary on Monday?" Leo asked, his voice concerned. "Are you going to be okay?"

"I'll be fine. I'll have some serious decisions to make that will distract me," I told him with a small smile. "I thought I'd be job hunting, but maybe not…"

"You can start sooner if you need a paycheck, but your physical presence won't be critical right away," he offered.

"I'm okay," I shared, touched that he considered my financial situation. Most people as wealthy as him probably wouldn't. "My parents weren't rich, but I had some money to bank once I sold my childhood home, and I've been able to save while I was at the sanctuary. I was lucky that I finished school with no student debt. I was comfortable enough to quit the sanctuary without another job. I need to work, but I have time. Honestly, I think it might do me some good to take a little time off. Today has reminded me of how much fun it is to just take some time to relax once in a while."

I'd been trying to outrun my pain and sadness for so long that I'd actually forgotten exactly how to slow down.

For the first time, I was also recognizing the fact that I could talk about the good times with my family without experiencing the blinding pain of their loss.

"I'd be ecstatic if you're interested in spending some of that free time with me," he said hopefully.

Being with Leo Lancaster was getting addictive, and it was a habit I really didn't want to quit, so I replied, "If you have some spare time, I can't think of anywhere else I'd rather be."

CHAPTER 11

Leo

MACY: *I THINK Hunter is missing you. He's been pouting all week. I hate you for feeding him steak and letting him play with the water coming from the faucet.*

I grinned as I looked at Macy's text because I knew she was joking.

Leo: *Bring him down this weekend and I'll straighten him out. How's everything going at the sanctuary?*

Bloody hell! I missed her beautiful face and it had only been a few days since she left last Sunday.

Now, it was Wednesday night, and I'd been lying in bed wishing like hell she was here when she'd texted.

We were in touch every day, either by phone or text.

So far, she said she was doing okay with her last week at the sanctuary, but I was still worried about her.

I doubted it was easy for her to see Karma's empty enclosure and not be melancholy about it.

How could she not be?

Macy: *Long day. One of our leopards has been sick, but he's doing better now.*

Leo: *How are you doing?*

Macy: *Hanging in there.*

Leo: *I'll think of some way to make you feel better when you come here this weekend.*

Macy: *Leo, I've been thinking about this and I'm not sure it's a good idea for me to come there every weekend.*

Oh, hell no. She couldn't back out on me now.

Obviously, she was thinking way too hard and had talked herself out of spending some of her free time with me.

Not going to happen, beautiful.

I clicked on her number and called her.

"What do you mean it's not a good idea to spend every weekend together? I think it's an excellent idea. Weekdays too, in fact," I told her as soon as she answered.

Macy sighed. "I just have a lot to think about and I don't want you to feel like you have to entertain me all the time."

"I don't," I said bluntly. "I'm the one who asked you to spend some time with me, remember? I want you here, but if you're tired of doing the drive, I'll come to you. It really doesn't matter."

I wanted to be with her. Period. I didn't give a shit how that happened.

"It's not that," she argued.

"Then what is it because it's definitely not *me* who doesn't want to see *you*," I rumbled.

Hell, after some of those damn kisses the two of us had shared, she should know by now that I wanted to spend as much time with her as possible.

And it wasn't just about the fact that I lusted after her curvaceous body. Yes, I wanted to get her naked, but there was more to our growing relationship than just sex...

"We talked about this," she answered. "I suck at relationships, and now that I might become your employee things are really... confusing. I talked to Jaya. She sings your praises as a boss and you're right. Her background was similar to mine when she started at the center in England. She said you backed her up every step of the way until she felt like she fit into her role."

"So you're leaning toward taking the job?"

Fuck knew that was what I wanted, but I hadn't realized that offering her the job would make her hesitant to explore the insane connection and chemistry between the two of us.

Not that I wouldn't have offered her the position regardless of how I felt, but maybe my timing hadn't been quite right.

She released a loud breath. "I'll think long and hard about the job just as soon as I finish this week at the sanctuary."

I knew she had a lot on her plate and I didn't want to pressure her, even though I hoped she'd accept the position.

"Fair enough," I told her. "But what does the job have to do with us?"

"If we're...dating, that throws all kinds of conflicts into the mix, Leo," she said softly.

"No, it does not," I told her tightly.

It's not like I'd be her direct supervisor who could ever critique her skills. That wasn't possible since I wasn't an exotic veterinarian. She was a professional on a completely different level.

"It does," she argued.

"Who said we're actually going to be... dating?" I asked.

We were going to be dating, and hopefully more after that, but I was willing to try almost anything at this point.

As long as we ended up together, she could call it anything she wanted.

She snorted. "What would you call it? You did have your tongue down my throat."

Bloody hell! It wasn't like I didn't remember that!

My tongue wasn't the only thing I desperately wanted inside her. In fact, our kisses were pretty damn tame compared to my fantasies about Macy.

Truthfully, it wasn't just the sexual chemistry between us that I wanted to explore.

There was something else there with Macy, a connection I'd never experienced before…

"We enjoy each other's company," I insisted. "We like being together."

"We do," she agreed readily. "We're dating, Leo. There's no way I can lust after you like I do and *not* be dating you. This is nothing like hanging out with a friend. Not for me."

I leaned back against my headboard. "Not for me either, sweetheart. Wait! You lust after me? Why haven't I heard you tell me that before?"

"Because it's not something a woman tells a man she hardly knows," she answered, sounding exasperated. "But I'm not gonna lie, you're my number one fantasy right now."

"I'd like to be your only one," I said in a graveled voice. "Would you care to share those fantasies?"

"No!" she said hastily.

"Would you like to hear mine?" I asked huskily.

"About me?" she squeaked.

"Yes."

"Absolutely not," she snapped back. "It would make me completely crazy. Leo, that's why we probably shouldn't see each other every weekend."

I grinned because she sounded so flustered. "Because you won't be able to keep your hands off me? Do you really think I'd mind?"

"Would you let me touch you any way I wanted?" she said breathlessly.

Fuck! The hopeful note in her voice nearly killed me.

A few seconds later she added, "Forget I just asked that."

"You can't take it back just like that," I told her. "It's the sexiest offer I've heard in years."

She snorted. "I'm about the least sexy woman on the planet," she informed me. "I've never been a girlie girl, Leo. I was a tomboy from the time I could walk and talk. I'm pretty much allergic to dresses unless absolutely necessary, and I smell like the animals I treat most of the time. Unless you want to count my underwear, which nobody ever sees, I'm totally unsexy."

I swallowed hard. "Your underwear?"

"I have a thing for really nice, pretty, feminine underwear," she said in what sounded like a reluctant admission. "God, I can't believe I just told you about that. I don't wear it every day because there's no way I could buy enough sets of the expensive stuff to wear every single day. It's something I do when I'm not…feeling good about myself or when I need a boost. I don't wear dresses. I'm not in the type of professional job where I put on a nice outfit every day, and I really do finish every workday smelling like my patients most of the time. So I wear a beautiful set of underwear when I know it's going to be a rough day. Don't judge me. It's just a weird quirk."

I was silent for a moment as I let that information sink in. "Fuck, no, I'm not about to judge you. Anything that makes you feel good works for me. I just want a heads up the next time you're using that lingerie to improve your mood that day. My mind has just gone completely wild and my dick is so hard it's almost unbearable."

"My only sexy days are when I'm wearing a pretty set of underwear and that doesn't happen often," she said like her words were a warning.

Like my dick wasn't going to get hard every time I saw her, sexy knickers or not?

"No, they're not your only sexy days," I disagreed in a hoarse voice. "You're gorgeous every single day, Macy. Fuck! Don't you ever look in the mirror? It doesn't matter what you're wearing. You're absolutely stunning."

She was silent for a moment before she said, "You're completely insane."

"If I am, you've made me that way," I griped. "Now tell me we're going to see each other this weekend. I miss you like crazy."

"I miss you, too," she answered wistfully. "But I wasn't joking when I said I didn't do relationships, Leo. I sucked at them even before my parents died, but after my parents and my brother were gone, I just stopped trying. What's the point? Nothing lasts forever and it's painful to care that much only to have that something or someone you care about ripped away from you."

Fuck!

What Macy had been trying to tell me finally hit me over the head like a sledgehammer.

It wasn't that she didn't do serious relationships.

Her point was that she *couldn't* do intimate relationships because they scared the hell out of her.

Losing her family had hurt so damn much that she was terrified to care about anyone that much ever again.

I doubted she even completely recognized what her motivations were, but I could see them.

"I understand," I said. "We can take this slow, Macy. Alright, maybe we *are* dating, but there's no reason why we have to rush into anything. Can't we just spend time together and see where it goes?"

I wanted a lot more than that, but I'd settle for what she could handle right now.

Macy Palmer had lost her entire family in one fell swoop; a catastrophe that would have left most people completely broken. Yet she'd picked herself up and carried on because she knew that's what her family would have wanted.

Granted, she'd been trying to outrun that pain for years by staying endlessly busy and not taking on any new relationships, but she'd survived by using those coping mechanisms, so I could hardly criticize her methods.

I doubted that most people would still be as functional and warmhearted as she was after suffering through that kind of soul crushing loss.

While I did understand why she didn't want to care about anyone or anything new in her life, the fact that she'd adopted Hunter not long ago gave me hope that there might be a chance for me, too.

I'd just have to be patient and persistent.

I didn't care how long it took for her to let go of those old fears. I was determined to be there when she did.

"We'll still have that little problem of you being my prospective boss," she reminded me.

I grinned because I could tell that she was starting to seriously consider coming to Palm Springs again.

"You haven't accepted the job yet and I'm guessing you won't over the next few days," I told her. "Not a conflict with you coming this weekend."

I'd fight her argument about dating the boss after she accepted the position.

It really *wouldn't* be a huge issue.

She let out a long sigh. "Okay, I'll be there. Just remember that I already warned you that I suck at relationships."

I grinned wider at her disgruntled tone. "You've definitely warned me several times. I'll gladly proceed at my own risk."

Perhaps she hadn't accepted my invitation with quite as much enthusiasm as I would have preferred, but all that really mattered was the fact that she'd end up with me by Friday night.

CHAPTER 12

Macy

EVEN THOUGH I knew I probably shouldn't, I ended up spending the next two weeks with Leo.

And not just the weekends.

He'd convinced me that since I wasn't currently working, we could check out all there was to see around the Palm Springs area while we had the opportunity.

Actually, time had flown by while I'd acted as Leo's tour guide, introducing him to places I'd been in and around the Palm Springs area.

In exchange, he'd insisted on taking me out to some of the really good restaurants in the evening. One thing Palm Springs had in abundance was amazing places to eat.

We'd even gone back to Newport Beach for a few days so we could take a trip out on the water to scuba dive. I wasn't the expert that Leo was, but I'd managed to keep up with him.

I'd let him catch me for many more of his stolen kisses, but Leo hadn't pushed for anything other than those passionate make out sessions we'd shared.

In some ways, that had made it easier to spend more time with him than I'd planned, but it made things harder, too.

I wanted Leo Lancaster like I'd never wanted another man in my entire life.

He was simply…breathtaking. I couldn't think of any other way to describe him. He was beautiful and perfect, which should have been intimidating, but it wasn't because Leo seemed to think he was far from flawless.

He was oblivious to everything that made him so damn attractive.

He didn't seem to care that his brilliant blue eyes could reach into my soul every time he looked at me.

He didn't seem to care that his crazy, wavy blond hair had a mind of its own, which just made him look like a sex god who had just rolled out of bed.

He didn't seem to care that he had a body that made women do a double take everywhere we went.

He. Simply. Did. Not. Notice.

Maybe there were some guys who *pretended* to be modest, but Leo was genuinely, entirely clueless.

Probably because he was usually focused on something that had nothing to do with his physical appearance.

I let out a quiet sigh as I watched him work on his own laptop on the opposite end of the couch from me at his Palm Springs home.

It was interesting how comfortable we could be just co-existing in the same space.

That connection between the two of us had just grown stronger, but I felt like we were learning how to handle it.

I rarely guarded my words with Leo anymore, and I knew he felt like he could talk to me about almost anything, too.

Leo had been putting together some of his papers on his work, and I'd been doing some independent research. The two of us could spend hours working in his living room and just be content that we were in the same space. Occasionally, I'd share something interesting, or he'd share something he'd discovered. We'd talk about it briefly, both of us exchanging ideas, and then we'd go right back to what we were working on before.

The two of us were just that comfortable working in the same area, which was really unusual for me.

And…somewhat disconcerting.

I'd spent the last five years in empty living rooms and empty apartments because it was much safer that way.

It was almost scary how easy it was to share my space with Leo now.

Soon, I was going to have to make a job decision. I couldn't be unemployed for too much longer, and I'd eventually get bored to death, but this time that I'd spent with Leo had been almost—magical.

Problem was—happiness was fleeting and no one knew that better than I did.

I didn't want to get too comfortable with the sense of well-being that I always felt when I was with him.

Or the exhilaration I sometimes experienced when he walked into a room.

I didn't really *want* to feel that way.

"Bloody hell!" Leo exclaimed in a low baritone that made me startle.

"What?" I asked him as I looked up from my laptop.

Leo slid down to me and held up his computer. "Look at this? What do you see?"

I squinted as my eyes adjusted to the light level of his computer and examined the photo he was holding up.

"Cat tracks," I said confidently. "Four toes and the ball of the foot."

"Exactly," Leo said, his voice triumphant. "These pictures were taken near the base of the Lanian Mountains by a native biologist. It looks like more proof that the Lanian lynx probably still exists, Macy."

My eyes widened as I stared at him. "Do you really think so?"

He nodded. "I know so. It's definitely a lynx track and there are no other wild cat species in the country. Prince Nick sent it to me. I told him to keep it quiet for now so the entire world doesn't decide to show up in northern Lania to get pictures or a trophy animal that was thought to be extinct."

"Could that really happen?" I asked, disgusted at the thought.

Leo shot me a dubious look. "You'd be surprised. If a new species is discovered or an old species is found again, more than just the wildlife world is likely to be interested."

I nodded. "I suppose so. It's news. It's so amazing to think that the Lanian lynx may not be extinct. Does the prince want you to go to Lania?"

"He does," Leo confirmed. "How do you feel about a trip to the Mediterranean? The weather should be nice."

"Me?" I squeaked.

He nodded. "My team is busy on another exploration, but I don't need my team, and I'd like to do this quietly. If we can just get video or photographic evidence, we can help Nick figure out how to protect them. The first priority is irrefutable proof that these tracks are from the Lanian lynx. The only way to be one hundred percent positive is to lay eyeballs on the animal itself."

My heart was nearly beating out of my chest.

How long had I dreamed of doing something like this?

How exciting would this expedition be?

How many times in the past had I wished I could follow Leo Lancaster on one of his adventures?

I shook my head. "No. No, Leo. I have absolutely no experience with field work. I'm not a wildlife biologist."

He grinned at me and winked. "I have enough experience for both of us, and it's not like we're going into unexplored territory. It's well mapped. It's just remote because so few people live there and the area was torn up from years of rebel occupation. Think of it like you're going on a camping trip far away."

He set his computer on the coffee table and wrapped his arms around me.

Leo looked at me expectantly while I tried to think of some reason why I couldn't do something I'd wanted to do nearly my entire life.

I shouldn't.

But God, I wanted to go.

Maybe I wasn't a wildlife biologist who'd done a ton of field work, but I was an exotic vet, so it wasn't like I'd be completely useless.

I was decent at identifying various animal tracks, and I could definitely identify a lynx, even at a distance.

When would I ever get a chance to do something this monumental ever again?

"Don't think about it, Macy. Just come with me. Nick said he'd get a base camp set up for us, and that he'd keep the information secret while we look for proof," Leo said as he rested his forehead against mine. "Stop overthinking everything."

"I'm...careful," I stuttered.

"Maybe that's not always necessarily a good thing," Leo said drily as he pulled back to look at my face.

"It is if it helps me keep my shit together," I said nervously. "Don't get me wrong. I'm tempted. How could I not be? Opportunities like this don't just fall into my lap. They don't ever happen for me."

"The opportunity is already there," Leo replied hoarsely. "All you have to do is say you want to grab it. I'll keep you safe there, Macy. If I didn't think it was safe, I wouldn't have asked you to go. For the most part, we'll just have to set up trail cameras and do some exploring to see if we can get eyes on a cat…or two."

I gazed at him as I took a deep breath and let it out. "You do realize that you're offering me something I can't possibly refuse."

I was going to go.

There was no possible way I could turn down the chance to see a Lanian lynx that shouldn't even exist on the planet anymore.

He grinned. "Maybe I should be insulted that you're just using me to see a Lanian lynx, but I really don't give a shit as long as you'll be there with me."

I shook my head as I looked into his eyes. "You being there is part of the temptation, Leo."

The guy still didn't seem to understand his status as a legend at finding extinct wildlife.

His eyes searched my face as he answered, "I didn't plan on making any trips in the near future, but I'm glad this came up. I want to share it with you, Macy."

Tears suddenly welled up in my eyes.

"I'm not used to sharing anything with anyone, Leo. I'm not used to anyone caring whether or not I'm around," I told him tremulously.

He swiped the tear away when it fell. "Get used to it, sweetheart, because I'm always going to care."

My heart ached with a longing that I hadn't experienced in years.

I wanted Leo to give a damn about me, but it terrified me at the same time.

"I'm not sure I want you to," I confessed.

"You can't stop it from happening and neither can I," he argued as he lowered his mouth to mine.

As usual, my body responded to his touch instantaneously.

I opened to him, and he plundered, he devoured, he ravished until I was utterly wrecked.

He buried his hands into my hair and used that hold to position my head exactly where he wanted it.

The panic that had initially welled up inside me vanished.

There was always that brief moment when I was terrified of how Leo made me feel, but it got swept away in the passion that inevitably followed.

I put my hands on his powerful biceps, reveling in the pleasure of touching him.

It had been so long since I'd felt this kind of need. This kind of desire.

Honestly, I wasn't sure if I'd ever experienced anything quite like this. It was a madness that only he could induce.

"Leo," I said in a breathless moan as he finally released my lips. "God, you drive me crazy."

"Welcome to the party, sweetheart," he said right next to my ear. "My balls have been blue almost from the moment we met."

"They have not," I argued, amused by his comment.

He moved back, but kept his arm wrapped tightly around my waist. "They most certainly have been," he answered, sounding slightly disgruntled.

"You didn't even really notice me in England," I challenged him.

He lifted a brow. "You think not? I was always looking for you, Macy. Wherever you went. Right after the first time we met. Why do you think I came into the library at Mum's estate where I found you crying about Karma?" He didn't give me a chance to answer before he said, "You were missing, so I went to find you. I'm not sure I even recognized what I was doing back then, but I understand that urge to want to follow you wherever you go now."

I brushed an errant lock of blond hair back from his forehead as I said, "I wasn't really missing."

He shrugged. "Then maybe I just sensed something wasn't right when I hadn't seen you for a while. Maybe you weren't gone long enough for anyone else to notice, but I did."

"And you found me," I whispered.

"I was rather determined," he said with a grin. "You weren't in the habit of disappearing at any of the wedding events."

I wanted to ask him why he gave a crap where I had gone or why he'd felt the need to make sure I was alright.

We'd barely known each other.

We'd hardly talked.

I sighed because I really didn't need an answer.

He'd cared because he was being Leo…and I truly was glad he'd found me.

CHAPTER 13

Leo

"I'M SORRY, LEO. I had no idea what had happened to Macy last time we talked or I would have told you. Kylie explained what happened. It's completely fucked up," Dylan said as we chatted on the phone later that evening.

Macy and I had thrown food on the barbecue and eaten outside because the weather was still so warm.

While she'd stepped inside to get Hunter his dinner, I'd decided to call Dylan and let him know I was outbound on an exploration where I'd inevitably meet up with one of his old friends.

I took a sip of my beer and put it back on the side table. "What in the fuck do you do when your whole family gets wiped out?" I asked him.

"I have no idea," he answered. "I completely lost my shit because I thought I lost a woman who cared about me and an unborn child. I can't even begin to imagine how it would feel to lose everyone I loved."

"I think part of her just shut down," I mused.

"Can't say I wouldn't do the same," Dylan replied. "Leo, you need to be careful. This might not be a path you want to follow. For your sake and hers."

"It's way too bloody late for that," I told him. "She's not bitter, Dylan. She's scared, and I understand that fear, but I can't just walk away from her because she's wary. I'd be the same fucking way. She's the only woman I've ever felt this way about. Damian told me once that he fell hard for Nicole because she liked Damian Lancaster, the man, and not the billionaire façade that most people saw."

"I can say the same thing about Kylie," Dylan admitted. "Is that how Macy feels about you?"

"If nothing else, she does like the real me," I explained. "I don't think she gives a damn about my money."

"Then you're probably completely screwed," Dylan said wryly. "That's hard to find in our world. Honestly, Leo, I don't remember you ever really having a girlfriend. Like you said, it's been a long time. But I had a feeling that when you finally fell, you'd fall hard. I'm not really surprised that you're crazy about Macy. She's attractive, she's wickedly intelligent, and she shares your passion for wildlife. And I doubt she does give a shit about your wealth. She's probably more impressed with your work."

"She is," I confessed. "We don't talk about work all the time, but it's nice to have someone who shares the same interests. I offered her the position of medical director at the new center here. I think she'd be perfect for it. She was ready to move on from the big cat sanctuary."

"What did she say?" Dylan questioned.

"She's still thinking about it. I think she'll take it. She wanted a challenge and I think this will give her what she wants in her career."

"It will conveniently keep her close to you, too," Dylan pondered.

"That's not why I offered it to her," I protested irritably.

Bloody hell! Dylan knew me better than that.

"I know that," he said. "Leo, I know you wouldn't do anything that would jeopardize your center. I'm just saying it would work out well for you if you two end up together."

"Oh, we'll end up together," I told him firmly. "There's something there, Dylan. Some connection that won't ever let me let go. It's been there since we met."

"I understand that connection, believe me. Be patient with her, Leo. She's been through one hell of an ordeal. I know it happened five years ago, but maybe she's just starting to open that part of herself she closed off. Kylie says she hasn't even dated since she lost her family."

"I think you might be right," I acknowledged. "She's coming with me to Lania. I don't need a whole team, and I think it will be good for her to get away."

I was finally starting to see the dark circles under Macy's eyes disappear and the bleakness in her beautiful gray eyes begin to fade.

I was hopeful that getting away to Lania and experiencing something new would help her even more.

"Sounds like a good idea. Kylie said that she's been worried about Macy. She could tell the situation with Karma was tearing her apart. She said Macy never talked about her family after they died and Kylie and Nicole never pushed because they knew it was painful for her." Dylan said.

"Losing Karma did tear her up," I confirmed. "That's why I'm glad she's going with me to Lania. She could use the break. She talks about her family to me, not about their deaths, but all of the good memories she has of them."

"That's something," he replied. "Do you remember how hard it was to remember anything about our father that wasn't painful in the first year or two? It got better. Eventually, we could talk about the happy times. I hope that's where Macy is right now. It gets a little easier after that. Not that I can compare her situation with losing one parent, but the grieving process has to be somewhat similar."

I figured that he was right, but Macy's grief had been threefold with no one left to talk to about it. "So when will you and Kylie be heading back to the States?"

"If I get my way, we'll see you two here for another Lancaster wedding shortly," Dylan shared.

"You two set a date?" I asked.

"We're looking at venues and trying to get something nailed down."

"I'm happy for you, Dylan. You deserve to be happy after all the shit you've been through," I told him sincerely. "Have you heard from Damian? Is he back from the honeymoon?"

"He called me and said he wanted another week a few days ago," Dylan said with mock irritation in his voice. "I guess I do owe him, so I told him I'd cover him."

"How's Mum?" I asked. "I haven't talked to her this week."

"As busy as ever, and already hitting Kylie with strong hints for a grandchild," Dylan said drily.

I chuckled. "She won't even let you get married first?"

I wasn't surprised. Mum had started hinting about marriage and grandchildren since the time we'd all finished university. None of her sons had cooperated until very recently.

"You know how she is," Dylan reminded me. "You might not want to tell her you're dating someone right away."

"Luckily, you and Damian are closer to giving her that grandchild she really wants," I joked. "I'll make sure to give her a call to check in before I leave for Lania."

"Tell Nick he needs to get back to the UK more often. Did you see him at the wedding?" Dylan asked.

"I didn't recognize him at first since he was incognito, but yes, we did run into each other," I told him.

Prince Nick had tried not to make a royal fuss out of Damian's wedding, and he'd succeeded in keeping a low profile at the ceremony and during his brief visit to the reception.

"Tell him I said hello," Dylan requested. "I don't envy his job of trying to pull a previously war-torn country into the twenty-first century."

I shook my head. "It has to feel odd to him that he was essentially raised as a Brit and returned to his own country as a virtual stranger to his people."

"He'll adjust," Dylan said. "Nick is one of the most loyal, intelligent men I know. He wants to move Lania forward, and he will. It may take some time, but he's doing an admirable job so far."

"He's been really helpful in this situation," I told Dylan.

"I'm sure he'll be ecstatic to find an animal that he thought was extinct in his country."

"He's pretty excited," I agreed. "Apparently, the Lanian lynx was a national symbol for Lania and it was present on ceremonial costumes and flags at one time. Nick said that finding them again would be a source of national pride that would pull the Lanian people closer together."

"I hope you can find some cats that are still alive," Dylan said. "The tracks looked promising?"

"Really promising," I confirmed. "But we need eyeballs on it for identification."

"Be safe," Dylan advised. "I know the country has become a tourist mecca, but I have no idea what it's like in the north. Considering how long the civil war was going on in Lania, it could be a mess."

"We'll be safe," I assured him. "I wouldn't take Macy with me if I thought there was any danger. There are no apex predators there and the weather should be warm. The tracks were seen in the woods at sea level, so I doubt we'll have to travel far into the mountains. Nick said he'd make a base camp as comfortable as possible."

"How long are you going to be over there?"

"Not more than a week or two," I shared. "I have too much going on here to stay away for too long. It looks like I'm getting a breeding pair of critically endangered wolves in two months. I'll need to make sure we're ready for them."

I picked up my beer and polished it off.

"Will you open to the public like you did at your center here?"

I swallowed a mouthful of beer before I answered. "Not anytime soon. It will be a while before we have a routine, and it's important for breeding areas to stay quiet so the animals feel safe. Eventually, I probably will operate it just like the center in England, but it won't happen right away."

Once I'd gotten established in the UK, I'd opened for limited hours of viewing and education so the fees would help support the conservation center for generations to come. At some point I'd do the same here in the US and the rehab center and emergency services would get some support from the state. It was important for me to find a balance between education and the future existence of the conservation centers and the well-being of the current resident animals.

"Have I ever mentioned how proud I am of you, Leo?" Dylan said in a low, older brother tone. "It couldn't have been easy for you to chase your own career choice when it was so different from what was expected in our world."

"It was never that hard when I had an entire family who supported those choices, Dylan," I said huskily. "Not a single one of you ever made me feel like I was less than because I didn't want to be a co-CEO of Lancaster International."

I'd gotten my inheritance when my father had passed away, which had been well invested to keep multiplying, and I still owned a small, silent partner share of Lancaster. Personally, I couldn't be happier with the way things had worked out. Not every Lancaster needed to be involved in the running of the mega corporation.

"But it was expected by everyone else outside the family," Dylan mused.

I grinned. "I didn't give a shit about anyone outside my family. Don't think I never heard people talking about the youngest, barbarian Lancaster brother who did nothing but crawl around in a forest getting dirty with filthy animals. If you remember, our father used to say that it was hard to give a damn what people said if you didn't respect the ones who were talking. I knew what the elites were saying. I just didn't care."

Dylan chuckled. "People like that have way too much time on their hands. I'm glad you didn't listen."

"We were raised by parents who taught us not to pay attention to those things," I reminded him. "I'll take my happiness over fitting in with them anytime."

"Me, too," he agreed. "I think we'd all love to see you more often, but you being happy is all that really matters."

"The constant travel has been the worst part of the job," I assured him. "I miss all of you, too, but I'm not going to be traveling the world forever. Other than this trip to Lania, I'm not looking to do more exploration in the near future. With this second center, I'll be busy. I can send my team out and finance an exploration without being there personally."

"But will you wish you were there?" Dylan asked somewhat hesitantly.

I thought about his question for a moment before I answered honestly. "Maybe I will once in a while, but for the most part, I think I'll be content to focus on all of the other important parts of conservation that need to get done. I'll spend time at both of the centers and I may even decide to buy a home in England, too. I'm starting to enjoy sleeping in a real bed."

"Getting soft, are you?" he joked.

"Not exactly," I denied. "I'm just saying I wouldn't mind sleeping on something softer than the ground sometimes."

"Can't say I blame you," Dylan said sympathetically. "Stay safe on your trip, Leo."

The two of us hung up after our usual goodbyes.

Afterwards, I had to wonder whether Dylan was cautioning me to stay safe from the possible dangers of the Lanian forest or if he was actually trying to convince me to guard my heart.

CHAPTER 14

Macy

"I THINK I'VE READ everything I could find on the Lanian lynx, and I'm all caught up on the politics in Lania," I told Leo two days later. "Are you sure there's nothing I can do to help you?"

I was also packed and ready to leave the following morning.

And so excited I doubted very much whether I'd get much sleep.

We were leaving bright and early for the Mediterranean, and I was so antsy and excited that I could hardly sit still.

He grinned up at me from his place on the floor where he had all his gear spread out. He was making sure it was functional and ready. "You've already helped a lot. There's not much left to do. Fill me in on what you learned."

I rolled my eyes. I hadn't done much of anything at all. Plus, I was done and Leo was still working to get ready for the trip.

Yeah, I'd cleaned out the fridge tonight, and made sure the laundry was done so he didn't come back to stinky clothes that were half washed, but that wasn't exactly what I'd call *helping*. I'd done the same at my apartment the day before, and I'd dropped Hunter off for boarding at a facility I trusted.

I put my laptop aside and got into a comfortable position on the couch. "Like you haven't done your homework?" I asked Leo teasingly.

"Tell me anyway," he insisted while he tinkered with one of his trail cameras.

"They're beautiful animals," I said with a sigh. "The last recorded sighting with photo evidence was over thirty years ago. I was surprised to see that it was the largest of the lynx species. The males can weigh in at a little over eighty pounds. They're not a subspecies. They evolved on their own, separate from the four known lynx species, but no one really knows their origins or how they evolved on an island. At one time, they were numerous, and roamed over most of the nation. As the population grew, they migrated toward the less populated northern areas. I guess we know what happened once civil war started in that country. God, I hope they're still there."

I was really hoping this trip would be successful, not only because I wanted to see a Lanian lynx, but because it would be incredibly significant to our field.

Leo looked up at me as he said, "I really think there's a good chance that there's some population left. I'm just hoping there's enough genetic diversity for their population to rebuild. Things can get pretty ugly if there are only a few left and they're closely related."

I nodded. "I hope so, too. It's really sad that some of the animals that have gone extinct managed to survive for millions of years but they couldn't endure the human race."

"Someday," Leo said in a disgruntled tone. "People are going to start to understand that our fate and the fate of these animals are intertwined. If they start wiping too many species off the planet, ecosystems crumble and the world starts to deteriorate."

"They're making some progress on de-extinction through cloning," I mused. "Although I think it will take a while to get it right."

"And it will never truly be exactly the same animal," Leo added. "It's a fascinating field, but I'd prefer we catch the problem before the animals are gone."

"Me, too," I agreed wholeheartedly as I watched him mess with another trail camera. "Are the cameras motion activated?"

"Yes," he answered. "I'll set up a bunch of them and see what we can capture."

"You'll teach me to set them up," I insisted. "I'd like to do some of the work while we're there. You won't have any of your team. You'll need some help."

"Actually, I'm pretty lucky that Nick is so accommodating. He'll make me lazy. He's setting up the entire base camp, including battery power, propane, and everything else we'll need to be comfortable while we're there," Leo said.

"I saw some pictures of Prince Nick. He's young," I commented.

Leo nodded. "Dylan and Damian's age."

"Apparently, he's seen as one of the most eligible bachelors in the world. I wonder if it's the fact that he's young and incredibly attractive, a crown prince, or because he's filthy rich. Or I guess it could be a combination of those things," I joked.

"What did you think? Do you think he's attractive?" Leo asked, attempting to sound nonchalant.

But I knew better.

He wanted to know if I thought Prince Nick was hot.

"He's good looking, I suppose," I replied.

"The bastard can be charming when he wants to be, too," Leo grumbled.

"Are you trying to warn me?" I asked with a smile. "And I thought you actually liked him."

"Yes, I'm warning you," he said abruptly. "And if you think he's attractive, I'm not sure I like the bastard anymore."

I started to laugh. It started out as a short chuckle that got louder the longer I looked at his face. "Oh, Leo. Don't you know that there's no man that's more attractive than you are?"

He acted like he didn't realize that he was on that same list as Nick. Mostly likely, he didn't bother to think about that.

He grinned. "Then maybe I still like Nick a little."

Seriously. The man had absolutely no idea how heart-stopping he was.

I snorted. "I could ask you the same question you asked me not that long ago. Have you looked in the mirror lately? If not, you should. You definitely won the genetic lottery. You're the most handsome guy I've ever seen."

He grinned broader. "Okay, I suppose Nick and I can be friends again. Your opinion is the only one that counts."

"You're impossible," I said with an enormous smile.

"You're beautiful," he shot back at me.

Even though I knew his words were far from the truth, it felt good to hear that, especially from a guy I couldn't stop lusting after.

"You're a lunatic," I told him. "If there's nothing else I can do, I suppose I should head for bed, although I'm pretty sure I won't sleep right now. I'm still too excited about the trip, and it's early."

"Then keep me company," he suggested. "I'm nearly done here. We can go out for a swim if you need to wear yourself out."

That sounded like a good idea. "I can do that," I said. "I also wanted to tell you that I've decided to accept your job offer. There's no reason to hold up on giving you an official answer. I don't know what to say about you giving me this opportunity, Leo. All I can say is that I'll do my best to make sure you don't regret it."

"I'm not even going to pretend like I'm not pleased," Leo answered as he started to put his equipment into a couple of backpacks. "And I'm never going to regret offering you the position, Macy."

"Jaya said she'd come over," I informed Leo. "But I think I'll be okay if I can FaceTime and videoconference. I'm not worried about the medical part of the job. I'm just hesitant about the captive breeding, and if you're really bringing in species experts, I think I'll be fine."

"Jaya might be disappointed," Leo said, his tone filled with amusement.

I frowned. "Why?"

"She's been wanting to visit the States for as long as I can remember. She hasn't gotten here yet."

"Whoops!" I exclaimed. "Maybe I should change my mind about needing her here in person."

"It might be the only way she gets here to see the US," he told me. "I can't seem to get her to take a vacation from the center very often."

"Then maybe you should leave it up to her," I suggested. "I was just trying to save her the trouble of coming here. Honestly, I am nervous, but it's an exciting new challenge at the same time."

"I think you'll love it," Leo said confidently. "We haven't talked about salary yet."

"I have a feeling you might pay a little more than the big cat sanctuary," I said carefully.

The money for my old job had been reasonable for a nonprofit that operated on a pretty tight budget, but it had been fairly low for a zoological vet.

While Leo still ran a nonprofit, it was a Lancaster conservation center, which meant cutting edge technology and salaries worthy of top tier professionals that were doing very specialized work.

Leo named a salary that left me gaping at him afterward.

It was nearly double what I'd made before.

"That's…really good," I said, trying to stop myself from sounding like a twit.

"No negotiating?" Leo asked teasingly.

"None. That's so much more than I was making at the sanctuary, Leo, and Jaya already told me about some of the amazing benefits."

"It's a lot of responsibility," Leo reminded me. "You'll be the medical boss of the entire center, Macy. The salary is appropriate."

I knew the pay would be good, but it was definitely more than I expected. "I may be able to afford a house eventually and give up renting," I considered.

I'd probably have to start out renting. Homes in this area were outrageous. I didn't really want to guess what Leo's home had cost him. Millions, definitely. I just wasn't sure how many millions.

Leo nodded. "You obviously have to give up your apartment and move here. Will you be okay giving up the beach for the desert?"

He sounded slightly apprehensive about what my answer would be.

"For a job like this one, of course I'm okay with it," I told him with a laugh. "I can get to the beach if I want to go."

In some ways, it might be good for me to start fresh in a place that didn't have quite so many memories.

Leo finally zipped his two backpacks and rose from his position on the floor. "I'm relieved that you've made a final decision, but don't think for one minute that we aren't still going to be dating."

I held my hands up in surrender. "I give up. I guess we'll see how it goes because I'm not willing to give you up."

His possessive gaze swept over me before he said hoarsely, "Brilliant. Because I can't possibly let you go. Are you ready for a swim?"

He held out his hands and I placed my hands into his without a second thought.

A few seconds later, he pulled me to my feet.

"How did I ever get lucky enough to meet someone like you?" I asked him softly as I met his beautiful ocean blue gaze.

Leo Lancaster was the entire package.

Smart.

Educated.

Kind.

Thoughtful.

Not to mention that he was also smoking hot with an amazing body that women lusted after.

There was also the crazy connection and chemistry between us that made me yearn for Leo Lancaster like I'd never wanted another man before him.

Every time he touched me, it drove me completely insane, but strangely, he also made me feel…safe.

Yeah. Well, that was pretty ridiculous considering that no one knew better than me that there was no such thing as complete safety.

Nothing was guaranteed, so it was better not to get too attached.

My problem with that strategy now was Leo.

It was hard not to want him, not to want to attach myself to him somehow.

I'd asked myself a million times now if I could sleep with him and stay somewhat detached.

Sadly, the answer to that question was probably going to be *no*.

Maybe if it was any other guy, I could keep my defensive walls in place, but not with Leo. Never with Leo.

"You met me because your best friend decided to make my brother the luckiest bastard in the world by marrying him," Leo replied to my question about how I'd gotten lucky enough to meet him. "It might have been a chance meeting that may not have happened any other way, so I'm fucking grateful that Nicole decided to forgive Damian for being an idiot."

I sighed as Leo leaned down and claimed my mouth in a kiss that told me just how glad he was that we'd met.

That same covetous embrace also conveyed to me that as of right now, he never wanted to let me go.

CHAPTER 15

Leo

LATER THAT NIGHT, my body tensed as I lay in bed, my brain somewhere between asleep and awake.

I opened one eye to glance at my bedside clock.

Two am?

I'd hit my bed around midnight. Right after I'd gotten myself off in the shower because being so damn close to Macy was making me completely insane.

Fuck!

I wanted to get her naked like I wanted to take my next breath, but since I wanted more than just sexual gratification, I knew better than to push her too hard.

I wouldn't trade those moments when she melted into my arms, but feeling that shapely body pressed against mine was getting to me, even though I kept telling myself to be patient.

I opened my other eye, wondering what the hell had woken me up.

I slept light from years of being out in the field, but I was usually out until I had to get up unless I heard or felt something that wasn't quite right.

I'd heard something…

My muscles clenched tighter as I heard the sound of my bedroom door slowly closing.

Is that what had woken me up? The opening of the door to my room?

The light was dim, the only illumination the moonlight in the room coming from the windows. As I turned my head, I realized the bedroom was just bright enough to see Macy's small form crossing the room, heading in a beeline for my large, king-size bed.

I not only recognized her small form, but the sleep shorts and oversized top she wore to bed. I'd seen them in the laundry several times.

I was facing away from the vacant side of the bed, but I could feel it as she climbed in, fought a little with the covers, and then moved as close to me as she could get without actually touching me.

So maybe I had initially been hoping that she couldn't handle another night in my house without being in my bed burning up the sheets with me, but it didn't take me long to realize that definitely wasn't the case.

I could hear her rapid breathing right behind me, and the vibration of her violent trembling.

I rolled over to face her immediately. "Macy? What's wrong?" I asked, trying to be as calm as possible, which wasn't easy since I wanted to make whatever had upset or scared her instantly disappear.

"I-I'm sorry," she answered, her body still shaking. "I didn't want to wake you up."

I reached out, pulled her into my body, and wrapped my arms around her. "What happened, sweetheart?"

Macy and I had been sharing this house for weeks now, and she'd never once felt the need to sleep anywhere except her guest room down the hall.

She snuggled up against me like she was trying to get warm as she answered, "B-bad dream. I haven't had one for a while, and I just reacted. I didn't want to be alone."

My gut ached with the knowledge that her first reaction had been to come to me, that she fucking trusted me that much.

I thought back to our evening together, wondering what might have triggered a nightmare for her, but I came up blank. "Do you want to talk about it?"

I leaned down and kissed the top of her head as she continued to try to burrow into me to get closer.

Her sweet scent was familiar and intoxicating, but I tried not to let my mind wander.

"Not really," she answered. "But maybe I should. I've had the same dream over and over since the day all of my family died. In that dream, I was there with my family that day. We went up in the helicopter together, and we're having so much fun. Dad was still cracking corny jokes when the helicopter went into engine failure. We were all holding hands as we plummeted toward the water. I know in that dream that we're not going to make it, but I'm okay with that because I feel like that's where I should be. I always wake up right before we hit the water and die."

My arms tightened around Macy instinctively. "Fuck!" I cursed. "Is that the same dream you had tonight?"

No wonder she woke up panicked and terrified.

"It was a little different this time," she explained in a tearful voice. "I was with my family, but for some reason, they pushed me out of our family circle at the last minute. Suddenly, it was just the three of them holding hands, and I was more of an observer. I was alone, watching them as the helicopter fell from the sky. As usual, I woke up right before impact."

"It's never happened that way before?" I asked her quietly, my mouth right next to her ear.

"No. I'm not sure what it means or if it actually means anything," she said. "This one was scarier than the others. At least I was still part of my family in the other dreams. Our fates were all tied together. That's the way it should have been, Leo. I was supposed to be on that trip that day. I should have died with the rest of my family."

"No, Macy," I rasped into her ear, my heart hammering against my chest wall.

I couldn't even think about Macy being with her family that day.

"Yes," she said in an insistent whisper. "It was a Friday, and I'd planned on being at that celebration. I ended up canceling at the last minute because we had an impending birth of a new baby western lowland gorilla, and I didn't want to miss the birth since it was so important because they're critically endangered. My dad was so supportive of me staying in San Diego until the baby was born. Even Brandon wanted me to stay and come to Newport Beach after it was born. He said we'd have plenty more celebrations together in the future and this one wasn't worth missing an event like that. But he was wrong. We were never together again. I should have been there with them, Leo. After the accident, there were so many times that I almost wished I had been there with them."

"Don't," I answered in a graveled voice.

Every muscle in my body tensed as I thought about how fucking close I'd come to never meeting Macy at all.

One lowland gorilla birth had been the only thing that had kept her from being in that helicopter.

Her survival had been a fluke, a really fortunate occurrence that had kept her from dying that day.

I took a deep breath and let it out, trying not to get lost in what could have happened.

Macy needed me to hear her right now. She needed to talk, and I was fucking here to listen.

"I'm glad you weren't in that helicopter," I said hoarsely. "I'm so damn sorry you lost your family, sweetheart, but I'm glad you're here with me now."

She let out a long sigh. "It was so hard, Leo. I was an adult, but I had no idea how to handle everything on my own. There were some relatives at the funeral, all of them from out of state, and none of them close enough to my parents to actually plan the funerals. My parents were high school sweethearts from Wisconsin. They moved to California without any other family around. My grandparents were all deceased, so it was just…me. They had a will, but no instructions for what to do if they were all killed together. I ended up putting them all to rest right next to each other in a cemetery that overlooked a pretty memorial park. I didn't know what else to do."

My fucking chest ached at the thought of a lost and alone Macy trying to figure out exactly how to bury her entire family.

Yes, she'd been an adult, but she'd still been so damn young.

I wished that I'd been there to try to protect and support her somehow.

"You did exactly the right thing, sweetheart," I assured her soothingly. "That's not a situation anyone can ever be prepared to handle."

I felt her nodding her head as she said, "I walked around in a daze, feeling so damn confused. A big part of me felt like I should be with them, and I wasn't even sure how to make myself leave the cemetery after they were buried."

I rocked her body slowly, trying to comfort her as I answered, "I think I'd feel the same way. How did you convince yourself to go?"

I sensed that she needed to talk and start to let go of some of those really brutal memories.

"Karma," she said flatly. "I remembered that I was supposed to be at the sanctuary volunteering. I went to her, and she kept me sane."

Thank fuck she'd had her tiger back then. Taking care of Karma had obviously steadied Macy enough to get through the difficult days.

Macy continued, "I had Nicole and Kylie, too. We mostly communicated long distance, but it was enough." She paused before she said, "I wonder why my dream suddenly changed."

I shook my head, "I'm not sure, baby. Maybe you're starting to believe that you really weren't supposed to be on that helicopter."

"I've been telling myself that there was a reason that I wasn't there," she shared. "I have to believe that Leo. That's why I forced myself to focus on the rest of my residency and being there for Karma and my friends as much as possible."

In my mind, there were plenty of reasons she didn't die that day, the main one being that the world simply hadn't been ready to do without her.

"Think about how many lives you've saved," I crooned to her. "Think about all of the important things you've done and still have to do in the future. Shit! Think about what a sad tosser I'd be without you. I need you, Macy, and nothing in this world is ever going to make me believe that we weren't supposed to meet."

I'd probably never meant a single statement more than that one in my entire life.

Macy Palmer was meant to be mine, and no one would ever convince me otherwise.

Maybe it was way too soon to tell her that.

Maybe it wasn't time for me to try to figure out the profound connection I felt with her.

Maybe I didn't completely understand *why* we were supposed to be together.

I just knew it was true.

"I'm sorry I woke you up, Leo," she said in a contrite tone. "But after that dream, all I wanted was to be close to you."

My hand fisted her hair gently and I pulled her head against my chest. "Did you really think I was going to complain about you slipping into my bed?"

She'd started to get the sad stuff off her chest.

She was talking to me about the hard things, the sad things.

At some point, she needed to work through the sad emotions and events that she'd stifled for so long.

I wanted her to know she could always come to me when she needed me, so I blew off any ideas she might have that her climbing into my bed was at all inconvenient.

Because it wasn't.

Not at all.

Even if she wasn't in my bed screaming my name while I fucked her.

She slapped my shoulder weakly. "You're a perv, so I'm sure you envisioned this situation happening much differently," she teased.

"When it comes to you being in my bed, I'll take whatever I can get," I quipped.

"Leo?" she said softly.

"Yes?"

"Thank you for always being here for me. Karma's death brought up so many emotions that I thought were over and finished. Like that crazy dream."

I had a feeling that Macy still had plenty of old wounds to heal, but I'd be there every time something new came to the surface.

She'd fought through all this alone for long enough.

"I'm always going to be here when you need me, Macy," I answered huskily.

"I hope so," she replied in a slightly fearful voice.

Maybe "always" and "forever" weren't really words she believed in anymore, but she'd eventually realize that I wasn't going anywhere.

"I feel better," she informed me. "Maybe I should go back to my own bed now."

"Sleep. Stay and I'll protect you if you have any more bad dreams," I said insistently. "We've got an early morning flight. Now that you're here, do you really think I'd let you get away?"

"Like I really *want* to get away?" she murmured sleepily. "God, you smell so damn good, Leo."

I nearly groaned as she buried her face into my neck and took another deep breath.

"Sleep, woman," I growled, knowing my patience was starting to wear thin.

I was a hairsbreadth away from groping her gorgeous ass and exploring every inch of her delectable body.

The only thing stopping me was the fact that she'd given me no sign she was ready for that yet, and I wanted her to trust me more than I needed to fuck her at the moment.

She sighed, and then her breathing slowed down as she did exactly as I'd asked.

She slept.

CHAPTER 16

Macy

"I CAN'T BELIEVE I'M flying for a second time on this beautiful private jet," I told Leo as I watched him finish our chess game by putting me in checkmate.

We'd been in the air for several hours, but we still had a long way to fly before we'd arrive in Lania.

He grinned at me. "Good game, but I don't think you were really paying attention."

I smiled back at him from my position on the opposite end of the couch, the chess board between the two of us. "How can I? I'm on my way to the Mediterranean to look for an extinct lynx. It wasn't like I wouldn't lose eventually. I think you're a nearly unbeatable player, and I'm mediocre at best. My brother and I just played for fun when we were younger, and I haven't gotten much practice since then."

"Should I assume most of your boyfriends weren't chess players?" he asked as he put the chess board back together.

I snorted. "You should assume none of them were interested in playing chess at all when we were in our undergrad. I managed to pull excellent grades, even though I was in a sorority and working a part time job, but the fraternity guys were all about the parties. After my undergrad, there was really no one long-term. There was vet school and any playtime I had was over. I told you that I haven't really had a steady boyfriend in a long time."

"Did you want one?" Leo asked in a curious baritone.

I tilted my head and thought about his question for a moment before I answered. "I don't think I really missed it all that much. Maybe because I hadn't met the right guy and I really was crazy busy after I started vet school. I tried dating for a while and then I just gave up. Most guys didn't understand a woman who wanted to put herself through so many years of higher education just to take care of wild animals. And there was nobody single and interesting in vet school with me."

"I would have understood," Leo answered soberly.

I lifted my head and our eyes locked across the chess board.

The earnest expression in his gorgeous blue eyes mesmerized me.

I shook my head slowly but didn't break our connection. "I didn't meet you back then," I said softly, feeling breathless and jittery.

"If we would have met when we were younger, I would have waited for you to finish school and all of your training. I would have rather had what little time we could manage together than be with someone else just because they had more free time," he said resolutely.

Jesus! If most other guys had said that it would have been a bullshit line, but not with Leo.

I completely bought his statement. Probably because his education had been important to him, too, so he understood.

"I would have waited for you, too," I murmured, still hypnotized by his gaze. "Well, if we had met earlier."

In some ways, maybe Leo and I had been waiting for each other. Him, in his studies in England.

Me, in vet school and then my residency.

Stunned by the thought, I suddenly broke our eye contact.

What was I thinking?

I don't do serious relationships.

I was casually dating Leo; I wasn't marrying him.

I was really physically attracted to him and I liked him a lot as a person. I enjoyed spending time with him.

I really needed to get things back into perspective.

We'd met by chance, we weren't *meant* to be together.

I watched as Leo put the chessboard back on the table made to hold the game before he came back to the gigantic leather sofa and sat down next to me.

He wrapped an arm around my waist and pulled me into his body, and I let him.

I loved the way he smelled.

I loved the way his hard body cradled my softer one.

I loved the sense of rightness I felt whenever he was close to me.

Maybe we wouldn't be together like this forever, but being close to this man was addictive, and wanting him was inevitable.

I came up on my knees next to him and wrapped my arms around his neck. "Kiss me, Leo?" I requested.

He lifted a brow, put his hands on my waist and lifted me over him until I was straddling him. "Maybe it's time for you to kiss me," he growled. "If you want something, come and get it."

Want *something?*

I wanted *him*, and he knew it.

I stared down at him as I asked, "Do you think I won't go after what I want? There's a million things I want when I look at you," I said honestly.

He spread his arms out wide. "I'm yours for the taking. If you see something you like, take it."

He was playing with me, and I was starting to like the game.

I fisted his T-shirt with both hands and bent my head down until I could feel his breath on my lips. "Like this?" I asked innocently before I boldly put my lips on his.

Leo participated, but he didn't take over like he usually did.

So, I kept on exploring.

I moved my hands to his gorgeous hair and threaded my fingers into the silky locks.

I gently bit his earlobe and whispered, "You're so damn beautiful, Leo. I like everything I see. Does that mean I can take it all?"

I sputtered as I suddenly felt Leo lifting my body and tossing me onto my back.

I was looking up at him on top of me before I could draw another breath.

He put his hands on the side of my head, and then he kissed me.

It was no gentle embrace, no teasing touch.

Leo took my mouth like it belonged to him and he'd been parted from it for a very long time.

He ravaged and pillaged with a ferocity that had me clinging to him, pleading for more.

"Leo," I panted as he released my lips and trailed his mouth over the skin of my neck.

Goosebumps formed on my skin, and I savored every possessive touch.

Something elemental between us had just done an enormous shift, but I wasn't complaining.

I'd wanted him for what seemed like forever.

"Yes," I moaned as I dropped my head back and let him have access to whatever he wanted.

I fisted his hair and hung on, gasping for breath as carnal sensations started to overwhelm me.

"Do you have any idea how badly I want to make you come right now?" Leo rasped next to my ear. "Or how badly I want to watch you while it happens?"

"No," I answered breathlessly.

Shit! I'd never seen Leo this earthy and carnal, but his desire seemed to feed my own need until I was panting with a craving I didn't quite understand.

I didn't protest as Leo grasped the hem of my shirt, yanked it over my head, and dropped it to the floor. "Bloody hell!" he cursed hoarsely. "Why in the fuck didn't you warn me that this was a mood boost day?"

It took a moment for my mind to function enough to understand what he was saying. "They're pretty tame today," I said softly once I realized what he was saying.

I was wearing a silky soft set of matching underwear. The bra was white with ivory lace flowers that were so thin they did almost nothing to cover my nipples. The panties were pretty Brazilian briefs that covered very little of my ass.

I'd wanted to feel feminine today, so I picked something that wasn't overly sexual, but sensual.

Leo traced my stiff nipples through the thin, ivory lace before he finally opened the front clasp and palmed my bare breasts.

I wasn't overly endowed, but they were a handful for Leo, which he seemed to appreciate.

"Fuck! You're so beautiful, Macy," he groaned right before he sucked one of the sensitive tips into his mouth.

"Oh, God," I moaned as he nipped and laved over the hard peaks with absolutely no mercy. "Yes."

He kept up the same sensual assault on one nipple and used his fingers to pluck and stroke my other nipple until I was nearly out of my mind.

My head thrashed on the leather, my body going up in flames as I wrapped my legs around Leo's waist. "I need you, Leo. I need…"

My voice broke off as Leo reached between us and popped open the button on my jeans and lowered the zipper as he said huskily, "I need to touch you, Macy."

I nodded my head eagerly. "Yes. Please."

I whimpered as he reared back on his knees so he could pull my jeans down my legs.

When they got to my knees, he stopped and simply stared. "Very pretty knickers," he said with a predatory look. "Do you have any idea how badly I want to tear them off and bury my head between your thighs right now?"

Oral sex had never gone all that well for me in the past. Most guys weren't thrilled about going down on a woman, but Leo's enthusiasm had me craving his mouth on me.

Leo slowly lowered the panties until he revealed my partially shaved pussy.

I'd left a small patch of curls as a little landing strip, but I was otherwise bare.

I shivered as the cool air wafted over the naked skin.

"Leo, please," I pleaded, my body on fire just from laying in such a vulnerable position while his heated gaze told me exactly what he wanted.

The same thing I needed.

I closed my eyes and shuddered. "Fuck me, Leo."

I sucked in a breath as I felt his thumb probe between my slit until he found my clit.

"You're so fucking wet for me, Macy," Leo said tightly.

"Then fuck me," I moaned.

He came back down and kissed me, his fingers still playing with my pussy.

I writhed beneath him as my tongue tangled with his, my hips lifting, begging for more than he was giving me.

My hard, sensitive nipples were still bare and abrading against his shirt as he finally released my lips.

I was so stimulated that I felt raw and incredibly needy.

"Leo, please. Please," I begged with not a single ounce of shame.

This man could play my body until I was senseless.

"Easy, sweetheart," he soothed right before his teeth nipped at my earlobe. "I know what you need."

"Then give it to me," I panted. "Now. Fuck me."

"I can't," he growled.

"Why?" I asked, my body shifting into a frenzy as Leo put direct pressure on my clit and started to give me the intense stimulation I was craving.

"Because if I fuck you right now, I'm going to want more, Macy. No more casual dating, no doubts about whether we should be seeing each other so damn much. We'll be in a serious relationship that's just about you and me and what we want. No more tormenting each other when we both know exactly what we want. You need to be damn sure that's what you want before you ask me to fuck you again. Because I can't do casual sex with you, beautiful."

My heart was racing as his words sunk into my brain.

I couldn't do a serious relationship.

I couldn't give him exactly what he wanted, even though I got why he was asking for that.

I understood the need for something *more* because of the crazy connection the two of us shared.

"Leo, I can't give you—"

"It doesn't matter," he said in a raspy voice.

He sped up his movements on the sensitive bundle of nerves he was fingering, and I felt my climax building with a ferocity that was almost scary.

"Come for me, Macy," Leo demanded in that sexy British accent that made me absolutely crazy. "I want to watch you. I want to see you take exactly what you want."

He was inviting me to grab whatever I needed, and I did.

I wrapped my legs tighter around his waist, lifting my hips until my core was pressed hard against his hand.

"More," I pleaded, my orgasm beginning to unfurl.

He gave me more.

His fingers stroked harder, faster and the pleasure was so intense that I imploded.

"Leo," I screamed as my short nails dug into his muscular biceps. "Leo, it feels too good."

"Never too good, baby," he said hungrily before his mouth came down on mine.

He gave me a rough, passionate embrace as my orgasm shook me, and then pulled back and watched my face as I came so hard that I wasn't entirely certain I'd live through it.

He didn't stop the intense stimulation on my clit until I finally started drifting down from my climax.

After that, he let his thumb tease the sensitive bud, wringing every bit of pleasure he could get from my body on the way down.

I laid there panting, unable to move as I tried to catch my breath while Leo murmured nonsense endearments into my ear.

He told me how beautiful I was, how sweet, how sexy, how perfect he thought I was.

And then, he got up and headed toward the bedroom with a quick, "I'll be back."

I heard the shower go on, and I instantly knew why Leo had gone.

I was completely sated.

It shouldn't have mattered that he was getting off all alone.

Yet there was an emptiness in the action that pierced the sensual stupor I'd been drowning in.

Jesus! I wanted to be with him almost more than I wanted my next breath, but could I make the commitment Leo wanted?

Mutual need wasn't the issue. If it was, I'd be right there and ready to go.

I was still asking myself that question when he returned in just a pair of boxer briefs, pulled my jeans and my bra off, and slipped my sleep shirt over my head.

I wrapped my arms around his neck as he lifted me up and carried me back to the bedroom.

I sighed as I cuddled up against him, knowing we had to sleep so we could jive our sleep schedule with Mediterranean time.

I heard the tempo of Leo's breathing even out as he fell asleep with his arm tightly around my body.

My body was satisfied but my mind was still busy, so it took me much longer than normal to follow him into a dreamless sleep.

CHAPTER 17

Leo

"YOU'RE CERTAIN YOU have everything you need to be comfortable out here, mate?" Prince Nick asked as we all stood around in our base camp. "It's pretty remote."

We'd arrived by helicopter fifteen minutes earlier.

Nick had surprised me by deciding to take the ride with us to northern Lania.

I definitely hadn't expected it after we'd had lunch with him and his father at the palace in the capital city where my jet had landed.

Apparently, Nick was taking this expedition very seriously, and he'd wanted to make sure that we were covered with everything we'd need.

I knew that Macy had been slightly taken aback about the necessity of a long helicopter ride.

Hell, I probably should have told her about that before she'd agreed to come along, but I hadn't connected the dots until I saw her face when Nick had mentioned the need for a helicopter because there was nowhere to land any other aircraft in this location.

To her credit, she'd climbed on board and held my hand so hard in the beginning that she'd nearly cut off the circulation in that limb.

Later, she'd seemed to relax because it was a large helicopter, and the ride was extremely smooth.

Eventually, she'd actually seemed to enjoy the trip.

"We're definitely set," I assured him.

Honestly, Nick had gone overboard, and we had way more than we needed and much more than I'd expected.

He'd erected two extremely large sleeping tents with ten-foot ceilings and plenty of room to walk. They were stocked with huge air beds, and small tables.

There were also several canopy tents with several long tables for equipment which would be perfect for a makeshift lab and a small kitchen.

There was also a camp shower and other amenities that I definitely hadn't expected.

"I've spent almost no time in this area," Nick said thoughtfully. "It was occupied even when I was a small child, and I've been so busy with everything happening in the capital that I haven't flown out here much to explore the north."

"It's beautiful here," Macy told Nick with a smile. "Thank you for letting me come here with Leo."

Nick shot Macy a charming smile back. "You're invited to anywhere in Lania as my guest anytime you choose."

I elbowed Nick as Macy strolled around the camp. "Take it easy on the charm, mate," I grumbled.

The little bastard simply grinned at me. "Feeling a little insecure, Leo?"

"None of your fucking business," I answered in a low voice so Macy couldn't hear me.

"Bloody hell! Stand down," Nick said nonchalantly. "I've never been a man who touches another man's woman. I just wanted you both to feel welcome."

"You've outdone yourself," I told him, feeling slightly less like I wanted to strangle him. "How's the tourist business going on the coast?"

"Better than I expected," Nick replied. "The beaches surrounding the city are some of the most beautiful beaches in the world. We're getting to be a popular destination for people who want some spectacular scuba diving and snorkeling, too. I knew nothing would happen overnight, but Lania is slowly becoming a very desirable tourist destination, which is really helping a lot of my people to make a decent living."

I nodded. "I'm glad your plans are going well."

I was happy that he was settling into his position, even though there were times it was hard to remember that Nick was a crown prince.

He was dressed casually in a pair of jeans, a polo shirt, and a pair of well used trainers on his feet.

He walked and talked like a normal Brit, but his actual title was far loftier than most of the titles in England.

Nick shrugged. "Nothing has exactly gone smooth. Not everyone accepts me as the crown prince because I was away for most of my life, but things are slowly getting better. I'm taking my place here no matter how long I have to fight to get the respect I want."

"Be patient, Nick," I advised. "People will come around. Lania has been through a lot of changes over the last several years."

"More than you can imagine," Nick muttered. "And I expected that I'd have to prove myself. During his rare lucid moments, my father thinks I should marry a Lanian woman with status to help things along, but there's no way I'm going to agree to an arranged marriage to help people accept me. It will happen on my accomplishments or not at all."

"Do they do arranged marriages here?" I asked curiously.

Nick shook his head. "It's definitely going to be discouraged under my rule, but it was a well-accepted practice in my father's generation. My parents had an arranged marriage. Luckily, they grew to love each other. I'm not willing to take that chance."

"Can't say as I blame you, mate," I commiserated.

"What about you?" Nick asked. "Am I seeing marriage in your future? It sounds like Dylan is ready to take the plunge. I just talked to him right before you arrived."

"Dylan will definitely take that plunge before me," I informed him. "Macy and I are still…figuring things out."

In some ways, I was still kicking myself in the ass for not taking what Macy had offered. She'd been completely willing to explore our physical attraction, but I knew it would never be enough.

Not with her.

Not when I wanted to explore a whole lot more than just a sexual relationship.

Not when I wanted more than just a fuck.

I knew what I wanted, and friends with benefits or casual dating with benefits wasn't even on my radar.

Nick clapped me on the back as he said, "You'll straighten everything out. If nothing else, you'll have some alone time out here. I mean, really alone. You do realize the closest thing around is a fishing village that is not a walkable distance away."

I shrugged. "I'm used to it. Just make sure you get back here to pick us up."

Nick nodded. "I'm off. I have a commitment this evening. You have the satellite phones if you need them. Good luck. It would mean a lot to me if you found the Lanian lynx. My people have lost a lot. Getting the lynx back would give Lanians something to celebrate."

"I'll do my best, Nick, but if I do get definitive proof, you need to be prepared to find a way to protect them. I can send my team over to help if you need them."

"What would that protection look like?" Nick mused.

"It all depends," I explained. "If there's a significant population, they may just need to be protected so they can repopulate. If not, they may need help recovering. We'll cross that bridge when we come to it. Right now, we just need proof that they're still alive."

Nick nodded. "Call me if I can help in any way."

Macy strolled back and we walked with Nick to the clearing where the helicopter was waiting.

I shook Nick's hand, and I gritted my teeth while Macy gave him a hug.

Fuck! I was losing it. I couldn't even stand to see another guy touching her, even when I knew it was nothing nefarious.

It didn't take long for Nick's helicopter to lift off and fly away.

"Well, that was an interesting day," Macy remarked as we started back to the camp. "I can't believe I just hugged a crown prince. Nick is a really nice guy and so down to earth."

"I'm sorry I didn't warn you about the helicopter, Macy. I didn't really think about the fact that you might be hesitant to fly in one because of the accident," I told her remorsefully.

She shook her head. "I've been in one before. It just took a little pep talk with myself to be able to do it again. Realistically, I know it's relatively safe to fly in one."

"Fear doesn't always vanish due to reason," I reminded her.

"I'm fine," she said firmly. "I'd tell you if I was still afraid to travel that way. When it comes to you, I just seem to open my mouth and say whatever I think."

I grinned at her. "I'm glad you don't hold back."

She rolled her eyes. "No worries about that."

"Then maybe you'll tell me if you're okay after last night," I suggested.

I'd been wondering all bloody day about whether or not she was okay with what had happened on the jet.

We'd gotten up this morning, showered—unfortunately not together—and then we'd landed soon after we'd both had our coffee.

We'd had company for the rest of the day, so this was the first time we'd really gotten to talk.

She turned to me as we reached the middle of our camp. "I think you know it was good for me. There's something there between us, Leo. I've never experienced this kind of chemistry. I'm just not sure how I feel about you getting off completely alone after you did everything possible to make sure I was satisfied. It wasn't a very fair exchange."

I was absolutely certain she'd known exactly what I'd done when I'd left her.

I just hadn't been able to stop myself from finding some kind of release, and I didn't trust myself when Macy was so willing to give me more.

Watching her come that hard had been pretty intense.

"What would you prefer that I do?" I asked.

"I'd prefer that you let me touch you," she answered. "I'd prefer you take me with you into that shower."

I clenched my fists at my side as I rumbled, "Do you have any idea what would happen then? I want you, Macy. I've never hidden that fact. I would have had your beautiful ass naked and up against the wall of that shower stall."

"And I would have been okay with that," she retorted hotly. "I've made no bones about the fact that I want you, too. I begged you to fuck me for God's sake."

Fuck! I was starting to second guess my decision.

Maybe I should have just let it happen.

Maybe we'd get so lost in each other that one of us leaving the relationship would *never* become an issue.

Maybe a commitment could come…later?

Bloody hell!

I hadn't wanted to plow ahead because I suspected that somewhere deep inside, there was still a part of Macy that was…fragile.

Maybe it was instinct because I'd seen how torn up Macy had become about Karma's death.

She'd also had my shoulder to cry on a time or two over the death of her family.

However, I suspected those events were nothing compared to the intense anguish that was still buried inside her.

Obviously, she'd never really allowed herself to fully grieve or deal with what happened.

She'd coped and survived, and I admired her strength, but I was hesitant to believe that she'd ever completely healed the damage the tragedy had done to her.

Hell, maybe I was completely wrong about that, but I wasn't about to do more harm by offering her nothing more than a satisfying fuck. Especially when I already knew I wanted more.

Had I screwed up?

Should I have just allowed the relationship to go however Macy wanted it?

"I think you should reconsider that decision," she said quietly before she walked toward the tents with her backpack in tow.

"Maybe you're right," I said after her retreating figure even though it was much too late for her to hear those words.

CHAPTER 18

Macy

I SPENT THE NEXT few days with Leo setting up trail cameras and exploring the general area where the Lanian biologists had located those tracks.

It hadn't been difficult to find a lot more tracks and other proof that the cats still existed.

We'd taken tons of samples of scat that looked very much like lynx poop, and we'd set up some hair traps as well, just in case we didn't get our eyes on a Lanian lynx this trip.

The hair and scat could be DNA tested to prove that the animals were still alive, pooping and dropping hair throughout the forests of Lania.

Granted, we hadn't yet spotted the cat itself, but I was full of hope that we would.

Like it was a silent agreement, Leo and I had put our tiff about sex behind us to focus on our mission here.

Leo slept in his tent and I slept in mine.

For the most part, our relationship remained civil and friendly, but not quite as carefree as it had been before he'd set me off like a firecracker.

Despite the underlying tension, I was lulled into a very good mood every day by the beauty of Lania and the extremely temperate weather.

"Look Leo," I said excitedly as I crouched down on the game path we'd been walking to set up more cameras. "More tracks."

He crouched down beside me to look at what we both knew were tracks made by the Lanian lynx.

"They're everywhere," Leo replied. "Not only that, but we've seen plenty of rabbits, so we know the rabbit population is healthy. It won't be long until we get eyes on a cat. Lynxes are solitary animals that only get together to mate, so it's encouraging that we're seeing so many tracks. I'm hoping that means different cats because the tracks all look like they're various sizes."

"We haven't seen any dens yet," I reminded him.

"Probably because we're following game trails to set up cameras," he answered. "Those dens are going to be hidden. They'll be far away from the trails that all of the animals follow to fresh water."

There was a small lake a mile or so away from our base camp, and we'd discovered game trails all over the foothills that led to that fresh water.

"You're right," I agreed as I straightened up. "I guess I'm just getting excited because we've found so much proof that they're here already."

Leo came up next to me with a grin. "Don't worry. We'll find them. This is probably going to be one of the easiest expeditions I've ever had. The signs are everywhere. We have to do all the groundwork first, but we'll start sitting in some blinds tomorrow or the next day to see if we can spot them directly."

I smiled back at him, my excitement almost palpable as I looked at how comfortable he appeared to be out in the middle of nowhere.

Leo was in his element, and it fit him like a comfortable glove.

He was so fit that he could probably hike for miles without breaking a sweat, but he never complained about waiting for me or slowing his pace to match mine.

He was wearing a pair of khaki hiking pants, hiking boots, and a long sleeved T-shirt that was a neutral color to blend in with the forest.

I was dressed similar since Leo had helped me pick what to bring along.

"We've found a good spot for every trail cam I brought with me," Leo pronounced. "We're losing light. You ready to head back to camp? After we eat I can put the Infrared drone up and see how much night activity we have in the area."

I was really interested to see that infrared drone in action.

It wouldn't tell us exactly what was out there, but we could guess on size and speed what animals we could be seeing.

I nodded as I started walking beside him, hating myself for Leo's somewhat standoffish manner.

It was my fault that he wasn't quite as unguarded as he'd been before we'd had that little disagreement about what sexual satisfaction should look like.

I'd second-guessed myself about my inability to agree to Leo's terms many times over the last two days.

Jesus! It wasn't like I didn't *want* to give him what he wanted, but there was a part of me that was still terrified to actually start calling this thing between us anything other than casual dating or even a friendship.

But honestly…wasn't it already…exclusive?

There was no other guy I wanted to date, and as long as Leo and I were seeing each other, there would never be anyone else.

In the first place, there wasn't another man on Earth like Leo Lancaster.

Secondly, he was the only guy I'd wanted enough to even try to date in a very long time.

So technically, it would be an exclusive relationship.

Was that enough?

Would it be enough for Leo?

Did he just want to know we were monogamous?

Honestly, I couldn't blame him for wanting that exclusivity, even though I was still stunned that he wanted that with *me*.

We weren't kids anymore, and I knew if I was sleeping with a guy, there was no way I wanted him to be with other women, too.

Did he really think there would be any other guy in the picture after he and I had gotten naked together?

That wasn't even possible for me.

Yeah, I could easily do the "no sharing" thing.

So why was I so hesitant to say so to Leo?

Oh, yeah. That's right. Relationships scared the hell out of me and I wasn't a long-term type of woman.

Apparently, somewhere along the way, I'd half forgotten about that when Leo Lancaster had come swaggering into my life.

I didn't want to just sleep with Leo and then just walk away or treat it like casual sex. There was a friendship between us, too, and that crazy connection neither one of us seemed to completely understand.

Apparently, he felt the same way.

So, why was it so damn hard for me to admit that?

I'd probably overreacted.

If his idea of a serious relationship was simply the two of us respecting each other and not seeing other people as long as we were in a sexual relationship, I could handle that.

"The camp shower should be ready if you want to use it," Leo said as we got closer to camp. "I loaded the water after I used it earlier. I think Nick left enough water to stay here for an entire year."

I wanted to groan.

It wasn't that I didn't want that shower, but I swore that damn camp shower hated me. I couldn't seem to get a decent stream of water that lasted for very long.

The water was warm because it was solar, and the warm temperatures and sunlight were in abundance here. Everything we could run on solar here did run on solar. The small camp stove and oven ran on propane, but even the tiny refrigerators we used were solar with a backup.

It was nice to have the ability to take a shower every day. The camp shower was just…a little frustrating.

"Thanks," I finally replied.

Oh, hell, I'd figure the stupid shower out eventually if there was a way to get more than a trickle of water from it.

It was a small issue in comparison to everything wonderful I was experiencing right now.

The mountain and forest views in Lania were breathtaking, and our search for the Lanian lynx was the most exciting thing I'd ever done.

"I'll start getting something together for dinner if you want to hit the shower. There's a few things in the fridge I can handle making on the grill," Leo offered.

Since there wasn't another soul for dozens of miles, there was no need for anything other than an open-air shower that was set up behind the sleeping tents.

"Okay, I won't take long," I told him as I started toward my tent to grab some clean clothing. If I was going to shower, I wasn't about to put dirty clothes back on my body.

The only way we could wash clothes was to do it by hand and use the Mediterranean breezes to dry them, but it worked.

After I'd grabbed something clean to wear around camp and a towel, I scurried to the back of the huge sleep tents and started shedding my clothes.

I'd gotten over any hesitance I'd had to be buck naked in the wilderness.

It wasn't like any of the animals in the area were going to pay any attention to my state of dress.

The warm breeze kissed my skin as I got naked. I wasn't about to complain that this particular shower had no stall. It was way too amazing to be surrounded by natural beauty.

As promised, Leo had filled the enormous shower bag to the top, and the tiny stream of water was nice and warm as I got my skin and hair wet.

I reached for the biodegradable soap and cleaned my body off first, grateful that Prince Nick really had thought of everything.

Once I was done awkwardly rinsing off, I was hesitant as I went to grab the biodegradable shampoo.

Rinsing my hair was probably going to be a little more inelegant and difficult than it had been to slowly get enough water to get the soap off my body.

I really needed a little more volume to do my hair.

Crap! I'm not taking a shower without washing my hair just because it's inconvenient.

I sighed as I put a dollop of shampoo into my hand and started working it through my hair. I wasn't about to run around with dirty hair for the next week or two.

I was just going to have to be patient with the whole process of getting my body and hair clean.

I hit the foot pump once I was lathered up and then engaged the nozzle.

Water trickled into my hair at a snail's pace.

"Shit! Shit! Shit!" I cursed.

Obviously, this was going to take a while...

CHAPTER 19

Leo

I WAS UNPACKING SOME wild berries from my backpack that I'd found near the lake earlier in the day when I heard Macy's loud, frustrated curse: *Shit! Shit! Shit!*

I wasn't sure whether to be alarmed or slightly amused as I dropped the last of the wild strawberries into a container.

When I heard a small shriek that followed her irritated curse, I decided I probably should investigate.

"Macy?" I called as I stood at the side of my tent. "Are you okay?"

"It's this damn camp shower," she said in an annoyed tone. "I can't get it to work right."

Yes, I'd seen her naked—or almost naked—before, but I wasn't going to stride into the middle of her shower if it wasn't okay with her. "Permission to enter?" I asked, unable to keep the humor from my tone.

She let out a long sigh. "It's not like you haven't seen it all before."

I actually hadn't seen *all* of it, but I wasn't about to dispute her claim.

I tried to keep the smile off my face as I rounded the corner and saw one of the most mesmerizing sights I'd ever seen.

Macy Palmer was beautiful when she was dressed.

She was even more magnificent without any clothes on.

I tried not to be a wanker by blatantly staring at her nude body, but it wasn't an easy sight to ignore.

"What's wrong?" I asked as I stopped beside her.

"The water stream sucks," she informed me. "I have a headful of shampoo and all I can get is a trickle. I don't know what I'm doing wrong. It's not like I can jump on the internet and troubleshoot."

She hit the foot pump and then held out the nozzle to show me what she meant.

Her eyes were still closed as the makeshift showerhead put out that tiny stream of water because she had shampoo streaming down her face.

Bloody hell! She was a gorgeous sight, even when she was frustrated with shampoo running down her cheeks.

I grinned as I took the nozzle from her hand, put my hand on her shoulder and guided her away from the foot pump. "Ready?" I asked.

"Yesterday," she answered drily.

I pumped the pressure in the bag up and held the nozzle over her head as the water came blasting out.

"Oh, my God," she moaned as she put her hands up and started rinsing her hair. "It is possible to get a decent stream of water."

"I'll keep the water coming and you rinse your hair," I suggested, trying not to notice what an amazingly curvy ass Macy had.

Alright, maybe I *was* looking, which probably did make me a wanker. I'd have to be a bloody saint not to get an eyeful of this gorgeous woman while I had the opportunity.

And I was definitely not ready for sainthood.

"This is amazing," she said with a groan.

"Why didn't you just ask me to help you instead of trying to take a shower with nothing more than a dribble of water?" I asked, still grinning like an idiot as I watched how much she was enjoying a real shower stream.

The holding bag was fairly large as far as camp showers went. She wouldn't be able to stand under there forever, but it gave a decent stream of water for long enough to take a quick shower.

"I thought I could figure it out," she answered in a disgruntled voice.

I was fairly certain she would have—eventually. "You needed more pressure in the bag," I told her. "All you had to do was pump it up more. A lot more, actually."

"That makes sense now that you've said it," she said as she threaded strands of her wet hair through her fingers to make sure they were rinsed. "Do you remember when I said I'd been camping before?"

"Yes," I said succinctly.

"I actually meant that I'd been camping…in a camper. A trailer that already had a shower included inside," she shared. "No biodegradable toilet paper, camp showers, solar power or air mattresses. Not that I'm complaining about the air mattresses because they're actually really comfortable."

I couldn't help myself. I threw my head back and laughed.

After I'd recovered, I said, "This remote camp is actually quite posh, but I'm sorry I didn't think about clueing you into some of the stuff you've never used before."

"For the most part, I've done okay," she said, her tone slightly defensive. "I guess I'm just not used to roughing it, but I'm not going through detox over my lack of a cell phone or television. I actually don't miss them."

I grinned as she started reaching around for her towel.

I handed it to her and released the nozzle so the shower shut off as I told her honestly, "You've done incredible for someone who isn't used to doing field work, Macy. Most people who aren't accustomed to being remote are antsy after the first day."

She wiped her face off and I saw her gorgeous gray eyes for the first time since I'd started helping her out with the shower as she said, "I honestly don't miss anything. This is such an amazing experience that I pinch myself a couple of times a day just to remind myself that it's real. I'm here in Lania with Leo Lancaster on a possible species rescue. It doesn't get much better than that."

"Unless you want to consider the camp shower," I teased her, unable to take my eyes off of hers.

She peered up at me sheepishly as she asked, "How many pumps?"

"Probably six or seven to start for this one," I said huskily, the intimacy of our situation starting to get to me.

"Whoops!" she said as she wrapped the towel around her body. "I guess I need a lot more legwork."

"I'd be more than happy to help you any time you need me," I informed her hoarsely.

"No need now that I know how to use it," she replied flippantly.

"Maybe I shouldn't have shared how many pumps it takes," I told her.

She actually flushed a light pink as she demanded, "Go so I can get dressed."

I turned around and started to walk back to our makeshift kitchen. It might have gotten my cock hard, but I'd thoroughly enjoyed that little interlude.

I still had no idea how to fix things between the two of us, but I was determined to figure it out.

Relationships were difficult for her, and it was understandable why she felt that way.

I should have been more patient, and approached things a little differently.

I shouldn't have put any pressure on her.

I should have waited and let things develop at her pace, even if it progressed at the speed of a tortoise.

Considering how difficult it had been just to get her to date me, it was unlikely she was going to want to date yet another guy, right?

Her big problem was commitment because admitting she cared enough to be in a serious relationship meant that her emotions were involved.

Fuck! I already knew that her emotions were involved, just like she knew mine were, too.

It didn't matter how long I had to do this crazy dance to finally make Macy mine. I'd bloody well do it until she was ready to tell me that there would never be anyone else for her. *Ever.*

Because I already knew she was it for me.

I'd found the one thing that was more important than my career. *Macy Palmer.*

She was the one woman I couldn't live without and I had no problem admitting the truth.

I'd find a way to work things out, because if I didn't, there *wasn't* another woman out there for me.

I knew that as assuredly as I knew my own damn name.

"Thank you, Leo," Macy murmured as she stopped, now completely dressed, right in front of me. "I feel just a little bit stupid."

"Don't," I ground out as I looked at her wet hair and her solemn gray eyes. "Why should you feel stupid when all of this is new to you? I should have offered to show you how to use everything. You are here helping me, and I knew you'd never been in the field before."

She smiled weakly. "I did profess to have some camping experience, but I've realized that there's *camping*, and then there's *really camping*. When you get so remote you have no cell phone, no television, no electricity, no gadgets of any kind, no toilets or running water, that's pretty real."

I smiled back her. "Welcome to my world."

"Would you really consider this posh?" she asked.

I nodded. "Absolutely. Getting a real shower every day or two is actually pretty huge, and we even have a kitchen grill instead of cooking over a fire. And refrigeration of any kind is pretty rare."

"And I'm sure you don't usually have air mattresses," she added. "But I appreciate Nick providing them."

"Not to mention more water than we're ever going to use because Nick flew it in," I added. "We usually split up the work when I have my team, but no matter how many hands we have, it doesn't usually get quite this good. It all depends on what supplies we have available and what we can get from nature. I found some berries earlier." I nodded at the container full of berries on the makeshift kitchen table.

Macy let out a gasp as she looked at the bounty. "They're enormous. Are those blackberries?"

"And strawberries," I told her.

"You never told me that you're a wild edibles expert," she scolded.

"You never asked," I replied jokingly. "When you spend a lot of time outdoors, I think it automatically becomes an acquired skill. We bring food, but it helps when you can supplement your food supply with nature, especially if the trip is really remote. Especially when you're trying to feed an entire crew all the time."

"I imagine there's only so much you can carry," she mused. "Especially when you need so many other tools and equipment."

"This time we really didn't *need* supplemental edibles," I answered. "But those berries looked pretty damn good."

Her eyes lit up, and she looked up at me and smiled. "They look amazing. Strawberries and blackberries are my favorite."

I'd hesitated earlier about wasting the time needed to gather up the berries.

We had plenty of food and I'd been impatient to finish setting up the cameras.

Now, I knew it had been worth every second it had taken just to see Macy smile.

CHAPTER 20

Macy

LATER THAT NIGHT, I didn't hesitate to crawl into Leo's bed as the thunder rumbled and the rain started to fall on the roof of his tent.

I had no idea why, but whenever I had the same recurring dream about my family, my first instinct when I woke was to find Leo.

He was easily found this time since his tent was right next to mine.

I wasn't sure if the thunder had woken me or if I'd just startled awake because I'd reached the part of my dream when I always woke up.

Leo's airbed was enormous, so I had to scoot across it before I was snuggled against his back.

"This is starting to get dangerously habitual," Leo said in an amused baritone. "Bad dream?"

"Same one," I said as I shivered against his back. "I'm sorry."

Leo rolled over and pulled me into his arms, no further questions asked.

I closed my eyes and savored the warmth his enormous, muscular body provided, and the way he simply gave before I even had to ask.

"I'm here. I've got you, Macy," he rumbled. "You never have to hesitate to come to me if you need me."

"It's storming," I said, stating the obvious.

"It'll blow over, and I'm definitely not worried that this tent won't hold up. Nick put up the best on the market."

"We've had such good weather so far," I murmured.

"It should clear up by morning," he said. "There was nothing but good weather forecasted and Nick would have called me on the satellite phone if it was anything serious."

"I'm not worried," I told him as I laid my head against his shoulder. "Call me weird, but I actually like the rain sometimes."

He stroked his hand over my hair as he said, "I probably wouldn't mind it if the rain hadn't washed out some of my exploration plans. It can be a pain in the ass."

"I suppose it could be," I agreed distractedly as I moved back a little so I could run my palms down his gloriously bare chest and over his ripped abs.

It was obvious to me that Leo was naked except for a pair of boxer briefs, and I needed to touch him so badly that I ached.

That particular dream always made me feel so damn alone.

Maybe that was why I always sought out Leo afterward.

He gently grasped my wrists as I moved lower.

"Careful, sweetheart," Leo said in a low, tight voice. "You're getting into dangerous territory and I'm not sure I have the patience to resist temptation tonight."

I tugged at my wrists. "Then don't. Let me touch you, Leo," I urged. "I don't like the way things are between us right now. I should have told you that I'd be okay with an exclusive relationship between the two of us. I wouldn't want you to be sleeping with anyone else, either. Why would I want to date or be with anyone else when I have you? I'm just hoping I haven't screwed everything up between us."

"You could never make me angry enough to walk away from you," Leo hissed. "And I know I made a mistake by insisting on more than you want to give right now. I thought I messed everything up. It's your call, sweetheart. I can wait, Macy, especially if you're willing to give us another chance. I adore you. Fuck! You must know that by now."

"I know, and I find that scary sometimes," I told him honestly. I really didn't understand what he saw in me when he could have almost any woman he wanted.

Leo pulled me on top of him with one powerful tug as he said, "Don't. Let me care about you, Macy. You've been alone long enough."

Something inside me melted. I craved Leo's affection as much as I feared it.

He let go of my wrists and I knew he was giving me the freedom to touch him all I wanted.

And God, I wanted...

I straddled him, fit my core flush with his rock-hard cock, and rode up and down his length, luxuriating in the intimacy of the motion.

"Bloody fucking hell!" he groaned.

"You're so big, Leo," I told him in an awed voice as I crawled between his legs and pulled his boxer briefs down his legs.

I tossed them aside, tugged my oversized sleep shirt over my head, and threw it over to join his boxer briefs.

I wrapped my hand around his massive cock and stroked him, reveling in the silken feel of the skin stretched over the steely hardness of the shaft.

"Christ! You're killing me here, woman," Leo rasped.

The tent was dark except for a small, solar micro lantern that was attached to the zipper on the door of the structure. Its light gave off just enough of a small glow so someone could see to get up and go outside if the need arose.

Luckily, it also gave me the illumination I needed so I could see what I was doing.

I swiped the small bead of moisture from the tip of his cock and tasted it.

I could feel him watching me as I bent down to take as much of him into my mouth as I could possibly handle.

As I released a hum of satisfaction, he groaned and speared his hands into my hair. "I'll spill like a bloody teenage boy if you don't stop, Macy," he growled.

I decided I really wanted to see and taste that, so I pulled back, let my tongue play with the sensitive head, and then doubled my efforts to go down on him harder.

"Fuck!" Leo hissed. "I've had fantasies about this, but the reality is better. You need to stop, baby."

Like hell I would.

Leo's pleasure was my pleasure.

I slid my hand up his thigh and fondled his balls gently as I bobbed up and down, allowing Leo to set the pace with his grip on my hair.

"So. Fucking. Good," Leo praised, his voice hoarse and incredibly sexy.

I wasn't exactly an expert on oral sex, but since he seemed to be enjoying what I was doing, I wasn't about to stop.

"Fuck! I told you I wouldn't last. I'm going to explode, Macy. Fair warning!" he said in a lusty baritone.

I sucked harder and faster, wanting to make Leo come more than I wanted anything else in this world right at the moment.

There was something about having the ability to make a guy like Leo completely lose it that felt enormously powerful.

I also wanted to give him as much pleasure and satisfaction as he'd given me on the plane ride before he'd left me to get himself off all alone.

He moved his hand from my head, presumably so I could move away, which wasn't going to happen, either.

I wanted to taste him and I did it greedily as he came.

"Christ, Macy!" he roared as I swallowed his release.

When the only sound in the tent was Leo's harsh breathing and the pitter-patter of the rain, I slid up his body and buried my face in his neck.

His arms came around me and held me against him, and I wallowed in the heady sensation of the two of us finally being skin to skin.

"You feel so good," I whispered against his neck.

He threaded his fingers into my hair as he asked, "What in the hell did you just do to me?"

I smiled against his skin. "The same thing you did to me on your jet."

"No, baby," he said huskily. "This was way better than that."

"Was that really one of your fantasies?" I asked curiously, suddenly wanting to know every fantasy he'd ever had so I could make them happen in real life.

He chuckled. "Can you possibly doubt it after seeing how quickly it was over?"

"I want to make you, happy, Leo," I shared.

"You make me happier than I've ever been in my entire life," he said huskily. "And that works both ways. I want to make you happy, too, sweetheart."

"You do," I whispered. "It's just been so long since I've let anyone get close to me."

He stroked a hand over my back. "I know, baby, but I'd cut off a limb before I'd hurt you."

"Then let's just focus on pleasure right now," I said in a suggestive tone.

Leo held my head in his hands and kissed me, rolling until he was on top as he ravished my mouth. "That happens to be my only objective at the moment," he said once he'd released my lips. "It seems I have you exactly where I've wanted you since the first moment I saw you."

I giggled. I couldn't stop myself. "I think you're out of commission for right now."

"Not for long," he warned as he explored the sensitive skin of my neck. "And not for what I have in mind right now."

My breath caught as he licked his way down from my shoulder to my breast. "Leo," I breathed, savoring every incredible sensation.

He palmed my breasts and lavished attention on both of them, taking his time so neither was neglected.

He nipped and sucked, teasing the sensitive, hard peaks until I squeaked, "Yes!"

I writhed beneath him, wanting more, needing more.

Like he sensed my needs, his big hand slid up my inner thigh until his fingers grazed over my soaked panties.

"You're already so damn wet, Macy," Leo groaned as he moved down my body and started to lower the damp panties down my legs. "Do you have any idea how much I want my head between your thighs so I can lick that gorgeous pussy of yours?"

"You don't have to do that," I panted.

No man I'd ever known had really wanted to go down on me.

"Please don't tell me you'll protest if I do," Leo said in a husky, completely turned on voice. "I'd be disappointed if you do."

"Most guys don't want—"

He tossed the panties aside and spread my legs wide. "I'm not most guys, and there's nothing I want more than to eat you until you come screaming my name," he insisted in a graveled baritone.

Jesus! When he put it that way…

"No protests," I panted urgently.

"Thank fuck!" he grumbled right before he buried his head between my thighs.

"Oh, God, yes. Leo, please!" I begged as his tongue invaded my pussy like he had to consume it or die.

My entire body shivered as he grasped my ass with one hand and pulled me toward his mouth like he couldn't get enough.

My back arched because the pleasure was so intense, and I buried my hands in his silky hair.

He licked from bottom to top over and over, making sure he didn't leave a fraction of a millimeter of my sensitive flesh untouched before his tongue started to circle my clit.

He was teasing, and I wasn't sure I could bear it. "More," I insisted as I fisted his hair. "Make me come before I lose my mind, Leo," I pleaded.

All teasing stopped and Leo laved over my clit with the stimulation I desperately needed.

I gasped as he inserted a finger into my channel without letting up on the titillation he was applying to that tiny bundle of nerves.

"Yes! Please. That feels so good," I moaned.

I felt my climax building.

"I'm so close," I panted, my entire body ready to shatter.

He sought and found my g-spot with his finger, and that was all it took.

He set me off, and my back arched up off the air mattress as I cried out, "Oh, God, Leo! Leo!"

I came apart, my climax going on and on while he kept up his sensual assault until I was completely spent.

CHAPTER 21

Macy

LEO FINALLY CLIMBED up my body and kissed me. I moaned as I tasted myself on his lips and tongue.

I was still trying to catch my breath when he released my lips. "Fuck me, Leo," I pleaded as I ran my hands down his back, knowing I'd never be able to get enough of his incredible body. "Trust me. There won't be anyone but you as long as we're together."

"I do trust you," he rasped into my ear as he reached for his wallet on the little table next to the air mattress. "Fuck! I'm sure I want this more than you do, but I want it to last. It seems I have no bloody control when it comes to you."

I saw him pull a condom out of his wallet before he dropped it back on the table.

I took the package from his hand as he went onto his knees, and then I sat up and opened it.

Leo was right there, between my thighs, as I started to roll on the condom.

"I think that you should have warned me that you were a sex god before all this started," I told him as I finished with the condom and tossed the wrapper on the table. "Do you honestly think I'm going to be coherent enough to time how long it takes you to orgasm? Because honestly, Leo, I'm going to enjoy this and I don't give a shit. It's been a long time for both of us."

I wrapped my arms around his neck and pulled him with me when I laid back down.

He brushed the hair back from my forehead as he said, "I've never wanted a woman as much as I want you, sweetheart."

I cupped his jaw and ran my fingers over the coarse stubble along his jawline. "Then show me, Leo. Please."

I gasped when he entered me with one powerful thrust. "Leo," I panted.

He was a big guy, and there was a moment of discomfort as my body adjusted to him.

"You okay?" he asked as he stayed still, his voice coarse and rough. "Fuck! I don't want to hurt you. You're so damn tight."

"It's nothing," I whispered. "It just took a minute to get used to you. It really has been a long time. I'm good. Fuck me, Leo. Please don't stop."

"Baby, you don't have to ask me twice," Leo answered as he pulled out and thrust back in.

"Yes," I said on a long moan.

He stretched me, challenged my body to accept him, and it felt so damn amazing.

I wrapped my legs around his waist and held on as he started a sensual rhythm that felt raw and elemental.

My body rose to meet his, both of us straining for the same intense, raw bliss that would send us over the edge.

"So good, Leo," I whimpered as my legs tightened around him. "Fuck me harder."

His pace increased almost immediately as he answered, "I can't wait to feel you coming around my cock."

A shiver ran down my spine.

He still sounded like he was in complete control while I was slowly losing my mind.

I bit his earlobe and then ran my tongue along the rapid pulse in his neck.

I could feel my orgasm building. I had no doubt that he was going to get his wish for me to climax.

As I smoothed a hand down his back, I could feel a fine sheen of perspiration covering his skin, which made our bodies slide together in the perfect dance. "Faster, Leo. Harder. You feel so good," I muttered mindlessly, my body primed and ready to erupt.

He started to pummel into me.

Harder.

Faster.

Hotter.

"Yes, Leo," I cried out. "It's-so-good-I-have-to-come-I-can't-hold-back-any-longer!"

I knew I was rambling, but it was about the only form of speech that I could handle.

"You're mine, Macy. You'll always fucking be mine," Leo growled as he moved his hand between our bodies and stroked a rough finger over and over on my engorged clit.

Hearing Leo's possessive words probably should have alarmed me, but they didn't. I instantly detonated, the orgasm I'd been anticipating hitting me fast and furious.

"Oh, my God, Leo!" I screamed as my body rocked with the most intense climax I'd ever experienced.

"Fuck, yes!" Leo groaned as my orgasm milked him to his own release.

"That was intense. So intense. So intense," I chanted as I started to come down.

Leo tightened his arms around me. "I've got you, Macy. I've got you."

Tears started to flow down my cheeks as Leo rolled over until I was on top of him and started to rock me gently as we caught our breath.

Maybe I should have known that if I lost control and went over the edge, Leo would be there to catch me.

But I hadn't counted on anyone except myself for so long.

He caught my lips, and gave me a long, sweet, tender kiss that made my heart ache.

"Are you crying?" he asked when he'd released my lips, sounding confused.

"No," I lied blatantly as I lifted my hand to swipe the tears from my face.

"You are," he corrected. "Why?"

"I'm not even sure," I said as I laid my head on his shoulder. "It's been so long for me, Leo, and it's never been like that. I haven't been to bed with anyone or anything except my vibrator for a very long time."

He chuckled and I slapped him on the shoulder. "I'm serious. It's just been me."

He ran a gentle hand up and down my bare arm as he replied, "I know, sweetheart. Same for me. But I honestly don't think I minded being alone until I met you."

"I don't think I thought I was missing anything, either," I agreed. "Until I met a guy I could only fantasize about before."

"The Indiana Jones of wildlife," he said drily. "Sweetheart, if anything, you're much too good for me."

I snorted. "Sure. Lucky you that you ended up dating a woman who adopts neurotic pets that are obsessed with flushing toilets. Leo Lancaster, you could have any woman you want."

He kissed the top of my head. "The only woman I've ever really wanted was you, probably because you're kindhearted enough to adopt the neurotic pets that no one else wants."

"I can't figure out how to use a camp shower, either," I reminded him jokingly.

"Now that," he said good-naturedly. "Will never, ever be an issue. I'll stand out there and hold it for you any day of the week."

"You're a pervert," I teased.

"Hardly," he responded. "There isn't a red-blooded male on the planet who wouldn't help a beautiful woman like you with her camp shower."

"I shouldn't need your help anymore. I know how to use it now."

"More's the pity," he replied with mock disappointment as he pulled out of my body and stood to take off his condom and shove his feet into his boots.

As he started to unzip the tent, I said, "Surely you're not going out in the rain just to dispose of a condom."

I couldn't see his face clearly, but I could hear the amusement in his voice as he replied. "I am. I'll admit that I'm not sure about the etiquette with condoms when you're out in the wild, but it must be somewhat the same. After what just happened, I'll gladly get wet to keep you thinking that you found yourself a great guy who doesn't make you share your space with a used condom."

I laughed as he unzipped the tent door and darted outside.

It wasn't exactly cold, but he was buck naked, and I could hear the rain still coming down.

Granted, I could tell that the rain had lightened up, but still…

Leo came back through the door a few minutes later, took his boots off, and dried himself off with a towel.

"I grabbed some water," he said as he handed me a bottle.

I sat up and took it. "Thanks."

I was actually thirsty, and I killed the entire bottle quickly.

He put his own empty bottle aside and got back into bed.

"Your skin is cold," I said with a squeaky laugh as he pulled my body snugly against him.

"I'll warm you back up," he promised.

I snuggled up to him, regardless of his slightly cool exterior. "What do we do if it doesn't stop raining by morning?"

"I have a few ideas," he said in a suggestive baritone. "And none of them include ever getting out of this bed."

"Do any of them include sleeping?" I asked.

"Overall, no, but maybe we can when we get tired. We'll probably have to eat occasionally, too," he answered.

"What do you usually do on rainy days out in the field?" I asked with a smile.

"I usually run out and pick up the trail cams so I can download them and scroll through all the times that they were triggered," he replied.

"But now you've got other ideas?" I questioned.

"Present company considered, hell yes," he grumbled. "We've got time. The trail cameras can wait."

I smiled and kissed his muscular chest, wondering when he'd last blown off work to get laid.

I was pretty sure that didn't happen often.

"Now you have me hoping for rain," I whispered.

He groped my ass and pulled me tighter against him. "We can make our own rainy day, woman. There's no one here to tell us that we can't."

I giggled and swung a leg over his body.

I wasn't about to argue with that.

CHAPTER 22

Leo

THE FOLLOWING SIX days were probably the best of my entire life.

I was on the home stretch in proving the continued existence of the Lanian lynx, but even better, I was doing it with the woman I loved.

Hell, yes, I knew I loved Macy Palmer. I'd probably known for a long time, but since I realized she wasn't ready to make that kind of commitment, I'd probably been in denial.

I was going to try not to push Macy for more, which wouldn't be easy since I knew exactly what I wanted.

I was going to hope she just needed…time.

Time to trust that I wasn't planning on going anywhere and leaving her all alone.

Time to discover that when you found the right person, it was worth taking a risk.

Time was on our side. For now, I'd happily take what she was giving, and worry about the rest later.

We'd taken some time off here and there over the last six days.

Once, to stay in bed for an entire day because we couldn't get enough of each other.

We'd also taken another day to walk down to the coast because I'd heard it was a sight too beautiful to miss.

It had definitely been worth the hike.

Today, we were working, and I hoped it was going to be the day when we finally laid eyes on a cat.

I'd avoided going through the trail cams because I was certain we'd have all the evidence we needed in those videos, with the scat and hair DNA as more indisputable proof. However, I wanted my and Macy's first glimpse of the Lanian lynx to happen in person.

It would be something special we shared together that we'd hopefully never forget.

"Oh, my God," Macy said with a slight cough. "That meat you put out in the clearing smells awful."

I grinned at her as I kept adding more foliage on top of the hidden observation area I was building. "That's the whole point. I guarantee it will smell delicious to a lynx."

I'd intentionally left the meat out to get ripe so the scent would help cover ours, and draw in a hungry predator.

She wrinkled her nose as she helped me put more dead leaves on the top of the blind. "I hope so because it smells rotten and disgusting to this human."

I chuckled. "It won't be so bad once we get into the blind."

"Do you really think we'll see one?" she questioned.

I looked at the hopeful expression on her face, which was a constant reminder of why I'd fallen in love with this woman.

Her heart was absolutely enormous.

"We already know they're here," I reminded her. "We've even seen some tracks leading into the mountains. I think we'll see one."

"I've got the camera ready just in case," she assured me.

Since Macy was a far better photographer than me, she'd been experimenting with her camera in low light since we'd gotten here. I had no problem with her taking all the pictures.

"I've got the stinky meat out," I teased as I glanced up at the sun. It wouldn't be long before the sun started to set.

I got Macy inside the blind with me and covered up both our scent and our bodies.

We were both absolutely silent and still as we lay there shoulder to shoulder, all of our attention on the clearing in front of us for the next twenty minutes as the sun began to sink in the sky.

My trained eyes scanned the terrain over and over with my binoculars, trying to catch a glimpse of something that I already knew would blend in well with the landscape.

Then, I saw it.

This lynx was enormous, which meant it was probably a male.

Even though I'd been doing this job for years, I still had that initial moment when I marveled at seeing an animal that was technically extinct. It was usually a minute or so that I soaked in the surreal emotions that surrounded the event.

Today, however, I was sharing that experience with Macy, so I gave her the subtle sign that I'd spotted a cat, a motionless pressure on her hand that she immediately noticed.

She didn't move.

She didn't say anything.

She just started searching more meticulously with her camera lens.

I actually felt the moment she spotted the cat as it moved closer to the odorous meat.

I'd done everything I could to wipe any human scent off that bait, so I was hoping the lynx took the opportunistic meal.

He moved closer, and I let out a silent breath of relief as the cat took his first bite.

I could see the stripes and dots on the tan fur, and once he was in the clearing, he was easy to identify.

He was close enough to see without the binoculars, but I kept using them, trying to assess the health of the animal.

From what I could see, he looked healthy and well-fed.

There was obviously a population of this rare animal left on the Earth. Nick would still have a lot of work to do to see how inbred and closely related these animals were, and how many were left, but there was hope they could be recovered if they were left in peace.

I looked over at Macy who was still quietly snapping pictures, and noticed a trail of tears streaming from her eyes.

I knew they were tears of joy.

Just knowing I could give her something that could make her this happy made this fucking fantastic day just a little bit better for me.

We watched, muted and motionless, as the sun completely set and the lynx quickly finished his meal.

Neither of us spoke for a moment, even after the cat was out of sight.

Macy was the first to break the silence as she whispered, "Oh, my God, Leo. Did that really just happen?"

"It did," I confirmed as I wiped the tears from her face.

"Now I know why you do this, no matter how uncomfortable it might get," she said, her voice awed. "That's probably the most extraordinary thing I've ever experienced. That animal is technically extinct according to the rest of the world. Thank you for sharing this with me, Leo. I'll never forget it."

"Who says we can't do this again someday?" I asked.

I planned on spending a lifetime with this woman. The opportunity would come up when we could do it again.

There would be another expedition in the future. Maybe I wasn't planning on doing a lot of traveling, but Macy and I could go occasionally.

Even though it was a tight enclosure, she managed to wrap her arms around me and hug me.

I held her for a moment, savoring the spontaneous affection.

"So what happens now?" Macy asked.

"Now the hard stuff begins," I told her. "Nick needs to get an estimate on how many animals there are, and probably dart some so he can check the genetics and health of the animals. If things look good, they might just need time to repopulate. They may not need any intervention except for tracking to watch the progress."

"He was so beautiful," she said as she backed up a little and held out her hands. "I'm still shaking. I'm assuming it was a male because of his size."

"I think we're thinking alike," I replied. "He was big, so yes, I'm assuming it was a male, too."

I carefully liberated myself from the enclosure and helped Macy get out of the small blind.

She started flipping through her pictures immediately.

"They came out really good," I observed as I looked over her shoulder. "You're a woman of many talents."

I took her hand and we headed back toward camp.

I'd leave the blind intact for now just in case we wanted to see the lynx one more time.

"What do we do now?" she asked. "We have a ton of pictures. Will we head back to California?"

"I'll have to collect all the trail cams and hair traps. We'll need as many videos and samples as we can get. I'll collect them tomorrow and we can head out the day after. We've gotten everything we needed here," I informed her.

I almost hated to leave.

I'd developed some very fond memories of this area.

"I'm excited to get to work, Leo. There's so much for me to learn at the center about the latest conservation techniques. It's going to really feel like a fresh start for me. A new city, a challenging new job, and a new and amazing guy in my life. I think I felt like I was in limbo for so long while I was at the sanctuary," she explained.

"Will you regret leaving Newport Beach?" he asked.

"No," she answered. "Now that Kylie and Nicole aren't living there fulltime anymore, I think I'm glad I'm moving. It won't really feel like home anymore without them."

Since her family was gone, too, that made sense.

I took a deep breath and forced myself not to ask if she wanted to skip getting her own place and just move in with me instead.

But I knew it was probably too soon.

I'd obviously been pushing it with the exclusive relationship demand.

Dammit! I was going to have to force myself to slow down.

Someday, she'd figure out that she owned my heart and that I'd rather die than hurt her, but now wasn't the time to tell her.

She had a lot of changes coming up in her life.

A new job.

A new city.

A new relationship.

I could at least wait until she was settled before I started campaigning for a whole lot more.

CHAPTER 23

Macy

"I HAVE TO ADMIT that I'm still jealous of these views," I told Leo jokingly two weeks later as we sat out on his patio after dinner. "I can't see much from my apartment balcony except concrete."

I'd made my physical move a week after we'd returned from Lania.

Because I'd found an apartment that would work for me in Palm Springs, and I'd paid for it, I saw no reason not to move as soon as possible.

I'd found myself a nice two bedroom on the other side of Palm Springs, but more often than not, I ended up having dinner with Leo.

He'd made sure that Hunter had everything he needed at his place, so I never had to haul anything with me if I wanted to bring Hunter along.

As promised, Leo sat in on every interview at the center for regular staff, and together we'd hired the best crew possible for the hospital and rehab center, which would be opening in two weeks.

He had professionals that were already working on the habitats for the captive breeding programs he'd committed to so far, but we'd worked together to hire some of the staff we'd need once the animals arrived, too.

Our days were busy at the center in preparation, coordination and paperwork.

We'd face a different kind of busy once the hospital and rehab opened, and we started receiving breeding pairs.

"That's all the more reason to spend most of your time with me," Leo replied suggestively.

I snorted and picked up my glass of wine from the side table of my lounger. "Like you don't already see enough of me between the center and the evenings I spend here?"

Leo and I were sitting in side-by-side lounge chairs that were so close we might as well be sitting in the same chair.

"Your office is on the opposite side of the center," he answered. "It's not like we hang out in the same place all day. It's barely daylight when you get into the office, too. You're working too many hours."

I took a sip of my wine and put the glass back down on the table.

He was right. We honestly didn't spend a lot of time together during the day.

Leo's job was to work with the various organizations on the conservation plans.

Mine was to get prepared to care for those animals once they arrived.

I saw more of Jaya via videoconferencing than I did of Leo during the day.

"I get in early because of the time difference," I reminded him. "I'm learning a lot from Jaya, but I have to make sure our sessions together are convenient for her."

By the time I talked to Jaya early in the morning here, it was already afternoon in England.

Leo reached for my hand and entwined our fingers together on the armrest of my lounger. "Then I'll bring her over to the US," he told me. "Macy, I didn't give you this position so you could kill yourself working twelve hour days every day. I don't wear my staff out that way. It's not healthy and it's not productive."

"It's just for now," I promised. "I want to make sure I get everything right."

I had my dream job.

I wanted to make sure I was ready for every challenge.

"We'll all do it right," Leo said firmly. "It's a team effort, Macy. Don't try to do everything yourself, beautiful." He hesitated before he asked, "Stay with me tonight?"

It was Friday night, so it would probably be easy for me to stay the night or even the entire weekend, but I wavered a little about giving Leo an answer.

It wasn't that I didn't want to stay with him the entire night, but the sex got so intense between the two of us sometimes that it was almost frightening.

At times, I needed to escape before I said or did something stupid.

"I may need to go into the office tomorrow," I hedged.

"It's Saturday," Leo reminded me. "Absolutely not. Unless the center is on fire or in a state of emergency, you don't work on the weekends. Bloody hell, Macy. You're putting in difficult hours during the weekdays already. What in the fuck is so important that you need to be there tomorrow?"

Nothing.

There was absolutely nothing important enough to necessitate my presence at the center the next day.

"I think I should go," I said as I got up from the lounger and grabbed my wineglass.

We'd had a really good night.

The last thing I wanted to do was spoil it by having some kind of disagreement about working hours.

Leo and I didn't argue, and I wanted to keep it that way.

Our relationship was warm but nondemanding. We had crazy good sex, and we could talk about nearly anything.

He followed me as I walked in through the sliding door and went to the kitchen to drop my glass in the dishwasher.

"If you don't want to stay, you can simply say so," he said as he leaned against the counter and crossed his arms over his chest. "You don't have to work like a maniac to avoid spending the night with me."

Was that what I was doing?

Probably.

But I really didn't want to admit that I was doing it.

"Why does it matter whether I stay overnight or how much I work at the center, Leo?" I asked, starting to get stressed out.

This wasn't the way things went for us.

Leo and I were dating as an exclusive couple, but we didn't really get involved in each other's business.

We had scorching hot sex, but I generally went back to my own apartment at the end of the evening.

We talked and bounced ideas and information off each other.

We did activities we both enjoyed together.

We worked together, but Leo had never put any restrictions on my position at the center…until now.

"Did it ever occur to you that I might just be worried about you?" Leo asked in an irritable tone I'd never heard from him before.

I turned toward him as I asked in a slightly panicked tone, "Why? I'm an adult, Leo, and I've been taking care of myself for a long time."

"Fuck!" Leo cursed, sounding angry now. "So we can fuck, but I'm never supposed to be concerned about your well-being?"

My heart began to race, and I could feel perspiration beading on my forehead.

I didn't want to argue with him.

"Things are good for us the way they are, Leo. You don't need to worry about me. I can take care of myself," I replied.

He advanced slowly as he said, "Are things exactly the way you want them to be right now, Macy? We have mind-blowing sex, but you usually don't stay long after that happens."

I started to breathe a little harder and my palms started to sweat.

He was right.

I did haul ass out the door, and the more fantastic the sex got, the faster I ran for the exit.

"I suck at relationships, Leo. You know that, and you knew that coming into this relationship," I said nervously. "I don't really understand why we can't just keep it simple."

It was easier.

It made more sense.

And it would avoid any kind of disagreements.

Leo crowded me against the counter. "I thought I was keeping it simple," he said hoarsely. "Have I asked you for anything?"

I shook my head slowly as I looked into his beautiful blue eyes. "No," I whispered. "Which is why I don't understand why you want to argue about my work hours or whether or not I spend the night here. I don't understand what you want from me right now."

"Because maybe things are a little too simple for me, Macy," Leo said in a growly voice. "And they've been getting a lot simpler as we go along. I've felt you creating as much distance between us as possible and I really don't understand why. I give a shit because I love you, Macy. I care if you work yourself too hard. I care if you aren't getting enough sleep. I care about every fucking thing that involves your well-being and your health. That's what happens when you love someone, sweetheart."

I blinked hard and my eyes widened. "You…love me?" I said in a voice so small it was barely audible.

He put his hands on my shoulders gently. "Are you really going to tell me that you didn't know that already?" he asked. "Are you going to say that you had no idea that I was hoping you'd marry me someday and put me out of my misery?"

My heart raced faster and beat so hard that I swore I could hear it thumping in my ears. "No, Leo," I said as I shook my head. "You can't love me, and I can't love you. We can't get married. Ever. I can't."

"Bullshit!" Leo said coarsely as he held my gaze. "I already love you, and marriage isn't a prison sentence, Macy. I know you're afraid, and maybe I sprang this on you too soon, but I think you care about me, too. I don't think you'd even be here in any relationship if you didn't. Don't tell me there's no chance for us at all."

"I. Can't. Love. You," I said in a stronger voice. "And I don't want you to love me."

"You *can't* love me or you *won't* love me," he asked gruffly. "Which one is it, Macy? We'll work on this together. I'll be patient. I just need to know that there's a chance of some kind of future."

I broke his hold and picked up my purse from the counter. "Nothing," I shouted, my entire body trembling. "There's no chance of anything. Don't you understand? I can't love you and you can't love me."

Tears were streaming down my face as I made that proclamation.

I could see the hurt in his eyes, and it completely gutted me, but I had to make myself absolutely clear.

I couldn't marry him.

There was no future for us.

I couldn't let him think that was a possibility.

He caught my upper arm as I raced for the door.

"I do love you, Macy," he growled as he turned me toward him. "I probably have since the very beginning. Don't run away from this. I know damn well you feel the same way I do. I'm not feeling this kind of connection all alone."

I jerked my arm away from him.

"It's nothing I can't get over," I told him in a desperate voice. "I can't do this anymore, Leo."

"Fine," he said tersely. "I can't make you love me, Macy. Drive carefully."

I scurried to the door. "I'll turn in my notice on Monday."

"Don't," he said in a graveled voice. "We can be professional. Like you said, we'll get over it. There's no reason to give up your job because of this. I'd like you to stay."

Tears were still streaming down my face as I nodded.

Unable to say another word, I opened the door and fled.

CHAPTER 24

Leo

"IT'S EIGHT AM on a Saturday morning," Dylan grumbled as he answered the phone. "This better be good."

"I just want to know what happens when you don't get the happy ending," I asked my brother as I poured myself another shot of good Irish whiskey.

It had been a housewarming gift from a colleague that knew I was buying a home in Palm Springs.

I thought I'd never drink it.

I was wrong.

"Leo?" Dylan asked, sounding more awake. "Bloody hell! I need coffee. What in the hell are you talking about?"

I heard a sleepy female voice which I assumed was Kylie, and Dylan telling her to go back to sleep as he apparently exited the bedroom.

I tossed back the shot, noticing that everything was starting to look a little blurry. "I want to know what in the fuck a man is supposed to do when he doesn't get the happy ending. When the woman he loves doesn't feel the same way. When she tells him there is absolutely no hope of any kind of future with him because she doesn't give a shit about him. Kylie loved you and you're getting married. Happy ending. Nicole loved Damian. Happy ending."

"Wait," Dylan said. "Let me guess. Macy doesn't love you and it's *not* a happy ending? What in the bloody hell are you drinking, Leo? You sound completely pissed."

"Irish whiskey," I told him. "Now tell me what happens when there is no happy ending."

I could hear the sound of coffee brewing in the background as Dylan answered, "What happened? It must have been bad to drive you to drink. I don't remember you ever getting pissed. I just talked to you forty-eight hours ago and you were nauseatingly happy about your future."

I filled Dylan in on what happened.

"I knew it wasn't going to be easy," I confessed to Dylan. "I suspected there was still part of her that had never healed, but I didn't know she felt nothing for me. Absolutely nothing."

"I suspect that once you get over your hangover, you'll realize that's absolutely not true," Dylan said wryly.

"That's what she said, so I doubt that," I said cynically, my words starting to slur.

"So, you're just going to let her go? Just like that?" Dylan questioned. "She runs away because she's terrified and you just turn your back on her?"

I glared at the current shot I was pouring, thinking about his question.

"Fuck it!" I snarled and I threw the damn shot glass against the wall and just picked up the bottle. It was easier. "She doesn't give a shit about me, Dylan. It's not like she was just holding back. She told me that to my face."

I'd heard her loud and clear.

"You're raw right now, Leo, and fuck knows I understand what that feels like. I understand why you want to put up your guard, but if you do, you'll regret it. You know where she's been, and you knew you'd come across some challenges, but I thought you felt like she was worth it," Dylan said.

"I did," I said hurriedly. "But there's no hope if she feels the way she says she does. I can't make her love me, Dylan."

"Let me ask you this," he replied. "I'm sure you're sleeping together. Do you really think she's a woman who can do that and feel absolutely nothing for you?"

I slammed my hand down on the table, frustrated. "A day ago, I would have said absolutely not, but after tonight I just don't know. Something happened to her, Dylan. You're right. She was probably scared, and I freaked her out because I told her I loved her. Hell, it never occurred to me that she didn't already know that. She'd just never heard me say it out loud."

"Do you think you saying that you loved her was a trigger of some kind?" he questioned.

"I think it may have tipped her over the edge. She was wild-eyed and horrified. I've never seen her like that. It was enough to destroy a man's ego," I grumbled.

I took a slug from the bottle and tried to remember exactly when Macy panicked, but the memories were getting dimmed by my intoxicated state.

"I think you need to stop chugging that whiskey and start thinking, Leo. You love this woman."

"What do you suggest I do?" I queried irritably. "She says she doesn't love me, and that we have no future."

"If it were any other woman, I'd tell you to run like hell," Dylan said. "But it's Macy, and we know her history. And whether you want to admit it or not, you know her heart. I don't think for a single fucking second that she doesn't love you back. She can't deal with how she feels. It's a defense mechanism that's worked for her in the past. She's just never learned how to let it go because it kept her sane. She doesn't need it anymore, but she doesn't consciously understand that."

I put the bottle down on the table. "How do you know that?" I asked, actually seeing that there could be some kind of truth in his words."

"Plenty of therapy," he said drily. "I'm starting to wonder whether Macy ever sought any help to get through what happened to her. If she hasn't, I don't doubt she's really confused."

Looking back, I didn't remember Macy ever mentioning seeing a counselor of any kind. "I don't think she did. Denial was her coping mechanism. Fuck! I probably should have suggested she do that."

"I think that's a decision everyone needs to make on their own," Dylan responded. "I'm not sure how much you're hearing me right now. I can tell that you're pissed and disheartened, but I sure as hell don't think you should give up right now. She might be pushing you away, but I don't think you should stay there. Give her some time. Make sure she knows you're there if she needs you, but let her figure all this out on her own. It has to be her choice to come back."

"And you think she will?" I quizzed.

"I honestly don't know, Leo," Dylan said solemnly. "But she knows exactly how you feel, so the ball is in her court."

"How do I stay available and let her know I'm there, but not push?" I asked.

There was no way I was letting Macy go this easily. Probably even before I'd called Dylan, I'd known that. I'd just been trying to get past my fucking wounded heart.

"You'll have to figure that one out on your own," Dylan advised. "It depends on what you think will help her. Once you're sober, think about it. In the meantime, toss out the rest of that bottle. You're going to regret that shit tomorrow."

Right now, I definitely wasn't sorry I'd opened the bottle because it helped to numb the pain.

"I don't want to live the rest of my life without her, Dylan. I knew from the very beginning that she was it for me. I'm not sure how I knew that or how I recognized it, but I just…knew," I told him earnestly.

"How long are you willing to wait?" he queried.

I shrugged. "Forever. I might lose my mind eventually, but there isn't another woman out there for me."

What did it matter how long I waited when there was no other female on this Earth that I wanted?

She'd change her mind or…she wouldn't.

The quicker she changed her mind the less time I'd spend as a totally miserable bastard.

"I understand," Dylan replied. "And it's probably going to be hell because there's nothing you can really do to resolve this, Leo. You have to let her have time to work everything out. You're not exactly good at doing nothing when you want something. I've seen you. You're driven. So it won't be easy to sit back and just wait."

"I don't think I have much choice."

"Think of creative ways to stay in the background," he suggested. "Now go and get some sleep so you can actually think. Sleep it off, deal with the hangover, and try to stay patient."

I stood, and my head started to spin. "Shit!" I cursed. "I haven't been this pissed in over a decade."

"Is the floor moving?" Dylan asked.

"Yes. And the damn room is spinning."

I stumbled, and then kept moving forward to see if I could make it to my room before I passed out.

Placing my hand on the wall, I used that to walk down the long hallway toward my bedroom.

"You still upright, little brother?" Dylan asked.

"Looking for my room," I told him.

I moved slowly, willing everything to stop spinning but it didn't happen.

"Got it," I told Dylan as I finally found my bedroom and flopped onto the bed.

"You safe now?" Dylan asked.

"Yes," I said. "Dylan?"

"What, Leo?"

"I wasn't thinking. All I could think about was how gutted I felt because she doesn't love me back," I said hoarsely.

"Just remember she has no idea how she feels right now. Maybe that will make things a little easier. Get some rest," he said.

"I'll find a way to make this a happy ending," I vowed as I crawled beneath the covers fully dressed.

"I'm sure you will," Dylan replied. "It's easy to want to bury your head in the sand and give up. I know because I've done that a million times. It never turns out very well."

"Night, Dylan," I said as I closed my eyes.

"Night, Leo," he shot back.

I'd barely hit the button to disconnect the call before I was out cold.

CHAPTER 25

Macy

I HEARD THE DOORBELL ring on Sunday morning, but I ignored it.

I didn't want to talk to anyone.

I hadn't slept much.

I hadn't eaten.

And I was in no shape to have a cordial conversation with one of my new neighbors.

All I wanted was to be alone and nearly catatonic on my sofa like I was right now.

That way, I didn't have to think about how I'd destroyed my life.

Blocking the pain was getting more and more difficult, so I needed to focus.

"Open the door, Macy. We didn't travel across the pond to stare at the door of your new apartment," I heard Kylie's voice boom from the doorstep.

I opened my eyes, wondering if I was starting to hallucinate.

I stood and walked to the door, and then asked carefully, "Kylie?"

"Yes. I'm here, too. Open the damn door," Nicole said, speaking for the first time.

I yanked the door open and saw that the voices of my two best friends were no hallucination. "What in the hell are you two doing here?" I asked, stunned.

Nicole entered first. "Thank God," she said gratefully. "I was already starting to melt out there and it's barely eleven in the morning."

"Me, too," Kylie said as she followed Nicole into the apartment. "I think I'd prefer the English weather right now."

Maybe that wasn't surprising since both of my friends were extremely fair. Nicole was a stunning blonde and Kylie was a fiery redhead. The scorching weather and ridiculously hot sun here in Palm Springs probably didn't agree with either one of them.

"I can't believe you're here," I said as I followed them into my kitchen. "Why are you both here?"

Nicole searched for the coffee, and Kylie filled the coffee pot with water as she said, "Because I have a wonderful husband with a private jet that can bring us over here at any time. Consider this an emergency intervention that we should have done a long time ago, but I think we all need coffee first. No offense, Macy, but you look like shit. Dylan told me what happened between you and Leo. He's a mess, you know. Leo called Dylan early yesterday and he was completely hammered, which is odd because Leo never gets drunk."

"Drunk," I said slowly, trying to clear my foggy head. "Leo was drunk?"

Nicole turned to me and shot me an assessing glance. "You really do need coffee," she decided.

I shook my head. "I still don't understand why either of you are here. I thought you were starting a new job, Nic."

"A week from tomorrow," she told me as she prepared the coffee. "I have some time to spend with a friend. I just hope it cools off here this week."

I raised a brow as I looked at Kylie.

She shrugged. "It's not like I won't be coming back and forth from the US to London," she reminded me. "Although I'm not here for work this time."

"Where are Damian and Dylan?" I questioned, still completely confused.

"London," Nicole answered. "Let's get some coffee and we'll talk."

Her tone was foreboding, but I tried to focus on how happy I was to see both of them as we all took our coffee to the living room.

Nicole dropped onto the other end of the sofa from me, and Kylie made herself at home in the recliner not far from Nicole.

I looked down at my sweatpants and T-shirt, knowing I looked like a bum next to the two of them.

I hadn't bothered to get in the shower since Friday, and I was fairly certain my hair probably looked like a rat's nest. "I didn't know you guys were coming," I mumbled as I sipped on my coffee."

"The trip wasn't exactly planned," Nicole informed me. "Kylie and I realized we needed to get here before you fucked up your entire life."

Kylie added gently, "If you give up your relationship with Leo, I think you're going to regret it, Macy. You love him."

I shook my head sharply. "No."

Nicole's voice was firmer as she repeated, "You love him. Neither one of us needed to see you to recognize it. You were in a relationship with him, which would never happen unless you were insanely crazy about him. Do you really think Kylie and I haven't noticed that you don't date at all since the accident? We're not blind to what you've been going through, but neither one of us ever wanted to tell you how to deal with a tragedy like that."

"But now we realize we should have pushed, tried to get you to slow down and stop running away from it," Kylie said. "And we should have tried to get you some professional help right after it happened. You seemed to be coping, but you really weren't. As your best friends, I wish we would have noticed that. Maybe we would have if we weren't all long distance. Once we all lived in Newport Beach again, you seemed okay, but you still weren't."

"You just learned how to hide everything better," Nicole observed. "We knew you worked too much, and when you weren't working, you were volunteering. Kylie and I understand now, Macy. You had to stay busy and exhausted or you'd have to deal with all the emotions you buried, right?"

"I like being busy," I protested.

Kylie frowned. "There's busy, and then there's so busy there's no time in the day to think. I should have caught what was happening before now."

"Me, too," Nicole seconded.

"I'm fine," I told them. "Things with Leo just got too intense. You guys know me. I suck at relationships. He was going to want more someday. He even mentioned marriage."

Nicole smiled. "It's not the end of the world, you know. It's actually like a new beginning of a different phase of your life. Hopefully a very happy one. You don't want to marry Leo someday? You love him."

"Stop saying that," I answered irritably. "He deserves better. I'm not capable of loving someone anymore. I don't want to love anyone else."

Kylie scrutinized my face before she spoke. "It's not that you *can't* love anyone. You *won't*," she deduced. "Because it might hurt too much."

Nicole held up a hand before I could speak. "That makes perfect sense, Macy, and I get why you blocked out that possibility after you lost your whole family. But is that really the way you want to live for the rest of your life? Leo loves you. He'd do anything for you. If there was ever a man worth loving, it's him, and I don't want to see you throw that all away if you feel the same way."

I was silent as emotions rushed up to meet me like a floodgate had opened that I could never slam closed again.

Tears streamed down my face as I answered, "I can't do it. I can't feel that way again. It would kill me."

Nicole moved across the space separating the two of us and wrapped her arm around me until my head was on her shoulder as she said softly, "It won't kill you, Macy. You're so much stronger than that. I know that life throws us a shitload of horrible things we have to deal with sometimes, but having someone love you like Leo loves you is one of the things that makes up for all the crap we get tossed at us."

Kylie had moved to the floor and was sitting near my feet as she added, "You've been there for both of us during our difficult times. Let us be there for you, now, like I wish we would have been from the very beginning."

"You have been there," I said tearfully.

"Not the way I wish we would have," Nicole replied. "We should have known better. We should have known things weren't getting better for you and that you were just barely coping by refusing to let anyone into your life. Well, anyone human anyway."

"I couldn't," I told them as I choked on a sob. "I still can't."

Kylie put her hand over mine as she urged, "You can. Maybe it was never time for you to do that before, but do you really want to give up on Leo?"

Sitting right in the middle of so much love from the two women who had been there for me since childhood, I finally broke. "I'm not sure I'm capable of giving him everything he deserves, and I have no idea why he loves me."

Nicole stroked my hair as she answered, "Just like I couldn't figure out why Damian wanted me, and Kylie couldn't understand why Dylan needed her. Love is never going to make sense, girlfriend. It's just there, and when it's the right guy, you recognize that click, that connection."

Kylie chimed in, "I'll be the first one to admit that it's scary, but once you get past that fear, you realize that taking a leap of faith is worth the risk. Are you really going to try to keep telling us that you're not crazy in love with Leo?"

I shook my head. I couldn't lie to them or myself anymore. "I love him. I love him so much that it already hurts so bad that I can't stand it. When he told me how he felt, I panicked. It was a kneejerk reaction during a panic attack because I've been so terrified of ever losing someone again. But I've already lost him and it's killing me. If I would have let him love me and if I had let myself love him, at least I'd have something more to show for the pain."

"I don't think he's going anywhere," Nicole said in a soothing voice.

"I hurt him, Nic. I think I hurt him pretty badly," I said, tears clogging my throat.

"Which sometimes happens when two people love each other that much," Kylie observed. "This is Leo we're talking about. He understands and if you explain I know he'll support you, Macy."

I lifted my head from Nicole's shoulder and started swiping at the tears rolling down my face. "If he does forgive me, I can't do this to him again. He deserves so much better."

"Which is why we're here," Kylie explained. "Dylan talked to Leo, and he agreed to give you the next week off. We found you the best counselor available in this area and you start sessions tomorrow. We have a spa day scheduled Tuesday, and we'll just hang out together for the rest of the week. Maybe you guys could give me some opinions on wedding venues. But the whole point of being here is just to talk. We'll never be able to completely understand what you've been through, Macy, but we'll talk like we've never talked before. Like we should have encouraged you to do from the beginning. You need to heal so you know this will never happen again."

I gaped at the two of them. "You're staying all week?"

They nodded as Nicole said, "We have to leave on Saturday so I can get back in time to start my new position, but until then, we're here to help you talk things out and lower your stress level. When's the last time you took time off for yourself and for your mental health?"

I shook my head. "Never. But I just started my job at the center. I can't just take a week off."

Kylie beamed at me. "Of course you can. We already cleared it with the boss."

"Leo," I breathed. "Are you sure he's okay with that?"

"What part of 'he loves you' don't you quite understand?" Nicole asked wryly. "He'd give you a year off if he thought you needed it. Don't argue, Macy. You need this. You need to get your head together and work through some things that you didn't resolve before."

I knew that there were things that had never been settled in my mind, and issues I still needed to work through if I had any hope of making a relationship work with Leo.

And God, I wanted that. I wanted him so much that it was killing me. "I won't argue," I told them. "I love Leo and I'll face any problems I have to work through for him."

"We're here to get you started," Kylie said with an enormous smile.

Tears flooded my eyes all over again as I looked from Nicole to Kylie, more grateful for these two women than I could ever express in words. "What would I do without you two?" I asked, my voice slightly shaky.

"Lucky for you, you'll never have to find out," Kylie quipped as she moved closer and pulled me down for an enormous hug.

I wrapped my arms around Nicole and the three of us stayed in that group hug until we were all in tears.

I heard my phone ping as we broke up our three-way embrace. "It's a text from Leo," I said as I picked up the phone.

Leo: *No pressure. I just want you to know that I love you and I'm here if you need me.*

It was short and sweet. Literally.

"He'll be there when you're ready, Macy," Nicole said gently. "He's not going anywhere. That's one thing I can say for Lancaster men, they're stubborn as hell when they want something."

I took a deep breath and typed a quick response back.

Me: *I love you, too. Give me some time?*

His response came back almost immediately.

Leo: *However long you need.*

I smiled as I ran a finger over his words.

I wasn't sure what I'd ever done to deserve a man like Leo Lancaster, but I was going to make damn sure he got a woman who appreciated him in the future.

CHAPTER 26

Macy

LEO: *HOW WAS your therapy appointment today?*
Me: *Brutal, as usual. It never seems to get any easier to spill my guts to someone who isn't a friend, but I know it's helping, so I keep spilling.*

I sighed as I made myself comfortable on the couch so I could chat with Leo.

It had taken several weeks for the two of us to start having full conversations.

He'd checked in daily, basically just reminding me that he loved me, and I'd made a quick response, but our conversations had just started a week ago.

My week with the girls had been an experience I knew I'd always remember.

Aside from starting my counseling that week, I'd also learned how to enjoy the art of doing almost nothing and loving every moment of it.

I'd felt better after that first week because Nicole, Kylie and I had done so much talking, and I'd improved every week after that from my counseling and altering my lifestyle.

I worked hard at the conservation center, and we were busy now that we were getting breeding pairs for the captive breeding program.

However, I'd also learned when to quit working.

Leo and I saw each other at the center, but we were extremely professional with each other, and there were no personal discussions while we were at work.

Yeah, there were times when I wanted to throw myself into his arms and never leave, but that was never going to happen when we were working.

Leo: *You're amazing.*

I took a deep breath and hit the audio call icon.

I knew that Leo would never initiate it because he was waiting for me to move forward at my own pace.

"I think you're pretty incredible, too, Mr. Lancaster," I said when he answered.

"It's good to hear your voice when we aren't talking about work," he responded in a sexy baritone I loved. "So your sessions are still a challenge?"

God, I'd missed him so much.

I was so ready to resume our relationship, but I wanted to make sure I was completely comfortable with the way that we loved each other.

Leo was a gift I never wanted to take for granted ever again.

"I doubt very much whether they'll ever get much easier," I told him with a sigh. "I really wish it was something that I started a long time ago."

"You're doing it now," he reminded me.

"I hurt you, Leo, and I'm not sure how to make up for that," I said honestly. "You didn't deserve it."

"Sweetheart, do you really think I can't take a little pain if I end up spending my life with you when it's all over?" he asked in an upbeat tone.

"People who love hard are going to hurt each other sometimes, I suppose," I replied. "And I love you pretty hard, Leo."

"Do you have any idea how long I've waited to hear that?" he said huskily. "And you're right. We'll hurt each other. It's inevitable. But I love you, too, Macy, and I think we'll both try to make the good far outweigh the bad."

"I don't think we can go back," I told him. "I think it would feel ridiculous because we were close before I managed to screw everything up. I think we can just do it differently. I'm always going to tell you how I feel when I feel it, and then we'll talk about it. I hope you always feel like you can do the same thing."

"So no more casual dating?" he asked hopefully.

"No. I love you too much for that, Leo. I also love you too much for the exclusive sex partners with no emotional involvement thing. I'm going to give you all the love I have and hope you're still in for a future together, whatever that looks like."

I heard him let out a long breath before he said gruffly, "I don't care what it looks like as long as we're together. Before we left Lania, I wanted to ask you if you'd just skip getting a place and come live with me, but I knew it was too soon. Date me and spend the night with me sometimes, come live with me when you're ready, marry me when you're ready to discuss that. It doesn't matter, Macy. As long as you love me, that's enough."

Was it really enough, though?

I didn't think so.

He shouldn't have to accept whatever I gave him.

It was time for him to get exactly what *he* wanted, and I needed him to know that this would be a partnership.

I smiled as I thought about the fact that words were cheap.

I was going to have to show him, and God knew I was ready to take Leo on new terms that were almost guaranteed to make us both happy.

"I miss you," I said in a breathless voice.

"*Meep!*" Hunter said loudly from his seat right next to me.

I laughed as I added, "I think Hunter is telling me he misses you, too."

"He only misses me for my multiple water faucets and occasional open toilet lids," Leo joked.

I stroked my hand over Hunter's silky head. "I still owe you a new Ficus tree," I teased.

"Not happening," he grumbled. "I think he's fond of the one I have."

"Love me, love my neurotic cat," I said with a laugh.

"Believe me, sweetheart, I do," Leo answered.

"Speaking of cats," I said. "What happened in Lania?"

"We don't have all the data in yet, but it looks like a small but healthy population. Most likely, my recommendation will be to monitor them and make sure the numbers keep growing," Leo answered.

"I'm so glad," I replied. "They have the habitat there to grow in numbers."

"They do, which is rare," he agreed. "They'll still have a critically endangered status but at least they're no longer extinct."

"Still the most amazing experience I've ever had," I shared.

"Then I guess I'll have to see if I can top it someday," he said. "I'll take you anywhere you want to go."

I smiled as I said, "That's a good thing since I'm starting to learn how to enjoy things other than work."

"Tell me," he insisted.

"I just did my second spa day," I confessed. "I really thought I'd hate it when I went with Kylie and Nicole, but it was pretty relaxing. I feel like a limp noodle by the time I leave, and my toenails are pretty."

"What else?" he urged.

"I'm starting to enjoy shopping. Don't ask me why. Maybe because I have a very generous employer who pays me well enough to make every day a mood boost day. I have every day of the week covered now with backup," I shared.

Leo groaned. "You had to share that."

"You asked," I reminded him.

"I wouldn't mind if I was actually around to see them," he replied. "Otherwise that's just cruel."

I giggled before I could stop the sound from leaving my lips. "You'll see them eventually."

"Promise?" he asked in a gruff voice.

"Absolutely," I agreed.

"It's good to hear you laugh, Macy," he said.

"I have a feeling it will happen a lot more often in the future," I answered, trying to reassure him that things would be different.

I was changing.

I was evolving.

I was handling my emotions like I should have learned to deal with them a long time ago.

Blaming myself for the way I handled that horrific tragedy in my life was pointless. I'd needed to get through the really painful years somehow, but it was time to leave some of those counterintuitive defense mechanisms behind.

"Thank fuck!" Leo cursed low and fiercely. "If I never see you cry again I'd be a happy man."

"No promises on that," I warned him. "I'll definitely do the happy tears sometimes. Kylie still has a wedding in the future."

"I might be able to handle that," he grumbled. "Bloody hell, Macy! I swear I'll spend the rest of my life trying to put a smile on your gorgeous face."

"All you have to do is walk into a room, handsome," I assured him. "You make me happy, Leo. Maybe that's why I panicked. Everything seemed too good between us. Sometimes I was waiting for the other shoe to drop because it seemed inevitable that something bad would happen just when I was really happy. I'm slowly getting over that expectation."

"Not to get impatient, and you can tell me to go to hell if you want to, but when will I see you, sweetheart?" he asked carefully.

I thought for a minute. "Saturday?" I asked. "I really need to go to Newport Beach. I have a storage locker I need to clean out, and I have another important stop to make. If you think you'll be around, I can stop by late in the afternoon at your place."

"What about Hunter?" he asked. "Are you taking him? You can drop him with me before you go to Newport Beach if you want. I'll be around working on a paper."

"Deal," I said happily. "He'd much rather be with you than me on Saturday."

"Then there's something seriously wrong with that cat," I said drily. "Because I'll always prefer to be with you."

"Just make sure your toilet lids are closed," I reminded him.

"I'm looking forward to seeing you, sweetheart, but you know how I am. I have a habit of pushing too hard. If I do, just tell me," he said in a sincere tone.

I smiled. "I promise I'll always let you know how I'm feeling from now on."

By the time Saturday rolled around, Leo Lancaster was going to understand just how done I was with holding anything back.

CHAPTER 27

Macy

"I'M SORRY, MOM," I said as I dropped a red rose into the tiny built-in bud vase on her headstone. "They were all out of blue roses today."

Blue roses had been my mother's favorite, but because they were dyed and cultivated through a genetic modification, they were rarer and weren't always easy to find.

Today, the blue rose had been a no-go after I'd checked three flower shops to see if they had any available.

Red roses were her second favorite, so I'd had to settle for that.

I sat down on the manicured lawn and put my hand on the cool marble of the marker my parents shared.

Brandon's tombstone was right next to my parents, which made it easier in my mind to talk to all of them at the same time.

I hadn't been here since I'd moved to Palm Springs, but today, I had some things to say.

"I wanted to tell you guys that I...met someone," I said. "I wasn't sure I could ever love anyone again, but I did. I do. I didn't want to, but he's so big, brash and beautiful that he was irresistible. Daddy, you used to tell me that someday a guy would come along that saw all of my good qualities. I'm not sure how that actually happened, but it did. No matter how hard I tried to push him away, he stuck like glue because he could see...me."

I reached up and swiped away a tear that trickled down my cheek.

I came here often when I lived in Newport Beach, especially when I needed to try to find some peace, but I rarely spoke and I'd never said anything about Leo while I was here.

Maybe I should have, because suddenly, everything seemed so damn clear to me.

Being unhappy, lonely and guarded for the rest of my life wasn't what any of my family would have wanted for me.

In some ways, I was here to live for all of them because they couldn't, and that meant being as happy as possible because that's the way we'd all lived when they were alive.

"I kind of think you all know about Leo," I murmured. "The dreams. I don't need them anymore. I get it. I'm not ready to die. I'm here for a reason. I'm here for him. I'm here for Leo. And he's here for me. I won't pretend that I understand all of the little nuances, but I get the big picture."

For some reason, Leo Lancaster wanted me, and I was done wondering why.

I *could* make him happy, and I was ready to start doing exactly that.

"I moved to Palm Springs," I told them. "I'm just here for a visit. I drove by the old house. It looks...different. The new owners painted it a pretty yellow color that I think you would have liked, Mom. There's another family there now making memories in that house, just like we made our memories when Brandon and I were younger."

I'd avoided going by my childhood home for years, but I'd deliberately gone there today. I'd needed to prove to myself that it was just a house, and that it was the memories that lived in my heart that were really important.

I'd seen that.

I'd finally realized that the house belonged to someone else and that they'd made it their own. But that didn't mean that I couldn't carry the happy memories of that house—when it was ours—along with me wherever I went.

I smoothed my hand over the stone as I choked out, "I love you guys, and I'll always miss you, but I know it's time for me to go live my life now. It's just been so hard for me not to feel guilty about living my life when you're all gone. And it's been way too scary until now to love anyone else. Until I met Leo. He's worth the risk, and I know a happy life with him is what you all would want for me."

I stopped and took a few deep breaths, my emotions raw as I swiped at the river of tears flowing down my face.

With every word I spoke, I felt lighter, so I kept on talking.

"I know you all would have loved him and all of his family, too," I said wistfully.

My family and Leo's would have had very little in common, but I instinctively knew that my parents would have adored Leo's mother, and Brandon would have really liked all of the Lancaster brothers.

"I won't be able to stop by as much because I'm living in Palm Springs now, but I kind of think you'll be okay with that. I'll come visit when I can," I promised them.

Leo would make special trips with me when I needed it, and I'd be back to Newport Beach to visit the animal shelter here that had been part of my life for so long.

It wasn't like I wouldn't come to visit my family's resting place, but I was ready to put more effort into my future instead of dwelling on the bad parts of my past.

I'd been hurting and trying to survive the emotional pain of my loss in every possible way for the last five years.

It was time to step out of that place of mental suffering and into my future with a man I loved more than I'd ever thought possible.

I didn't know what the future held for me, but it had to be better than the past five years had been.

"Thank you for everything you gave me," I said in a grateful whisper. "If you hadn't loved me, if you hadn't supported me, if you hadn't been there for me, I never would have met Leo."

My parents and Brandon had been there through so much of my long, arduous higher education journey. They'd gotten me through vet school and celebrated my internship and my residency.

Brandon had been there to push me every single day, whether it was by text, phone or in person.

My dad had always had the words of wisdom I'd needed.

And Mom had been a tower of strength that I'd sometimes desperately needed when things got frustrating or difficult.

"All I really want is to make you all proud. That's why I need to move on," I said, my throat clogged with emotion.

I suddenly startled when I felt something brush over the back of my hand.

I turned my head, certain I was going to find an ugly bug crawling over my fingers.

I froze as I saw what was really grazing my skin.

A blue rose. A perfect shade of royal blue, and as fresh as the red rose I'd just dropped into the bud vase.

I picked it up and looked around, trying to figure out where it had come from.

There were no other flowers blowing around.

In fact, there wasn't much of a breeze at all.

A sign?

Approval?

Some kind of signal that it really was time for me to move on?

Not to forget, but to celebrate the fact that I was, in fact, still alive and entitled to my happiness.

I really didn't believe in signs or the supernatural.

I twirled the rose between my fingers, reminding myself that I *had* recently started to contemplate the possibility of soulmates.

So why couldn't my family be sending me a symbol that would give me some peace?

Especially when that damn blue rose had suddenly made my heart feel lighter than it had been in a very long time.

I stood and brushed off my jeans before I carefully arranged the blue rose in the vase next to the red one.

"Thank you," I said in a heartfelt, hushed tone.

I kissed the tips of my fingers and laid them against first my parent's stone, and then Brandon's.

For the first time in five years, I was able to stand here in gratitude rather than guilt and intense sorrow.

"I'll always love you all," I told them quietly right before I turned and walked away.

I'd carry the happy memories in my heart so that a piece of every one of them would live on in me for the rest of my life.

But now, I had a man who was waiting for me, and hope in my soul that he was still willing to accept me.

I smiled as I got into my car.

I was ready to show Leo Lancaster that he wasn't the only one who could stick like glue.

CHAPTER 28

Leo

"BLOODY HELL!" I muttered in an irritated voice to Hunter as he lounged next to me on my sofa. "How the fuck long does it take to clean out a storage locker? I should have gone with her."

"*Meep!*" Hunter replied as he looked at me like he understood my frustration.

Hell, maybe he did because the feline probably missed her, too.

Macy had departed early this morning after dropping Hunter off.

She'd said she wouldn't be long in Newport Beach, but it was already after dark.

She's an adult.

She can take care of herself.

I'd resisted the instinct to text or call her since I knew she was busy and I didn't want to sound like a possessive wanker.

I needed to learn to back off and realize that Macy was perfectly capable of taking care of herself.

Then again, what if something had happened and her car had broken down on the freeway...

"She has five more minutes before I text," I said to Hunter in a warning voice.

The cat looked at me like he didn't care if I texted right now.

"Right. I agree," I told Hunter as I reached for my mobile on the coffee table. "We'll just make sure she's okay. That's all."

"Meep!" Hunter answered.

I probably could have asked more questions when she'd dropped Hunter off, like what time she'd be home. Maybe I just hadn't wanted to push her for an exact arrival time.

Me: *Just checking to make sure that you're safe. I wasn't sure how long it would take for you to finish in Newport Beach. Let me know.*

"That sounded casual enough, right?" I asked Hunter. "Not too pushy or bossy?"

He didn't answer this time. The cat was currently extremely focused on grooming his paw.

My body relaxed a little when a reply to my text appeared.

Macy: *I'm here. I'm outside unloading.*

"She's doing what?" I said aloud with a frown.

I sprinted for the door, not bothering to find my shoes before I stepped outside.

I observed from the doorstep, not able to say a single word as I watched her going back and forth from her car to the front door with armloads of items.

I folded my arms over my chest. "What exactly are you doing?" I questioned.

She dropped some empty hangers into the growing pile. "Unloading my stuff."

"I see that," I said, dumbfounded. "I'm just wondering...why."

She trekked back to the car and carried another box to the front porch. "The moving guys will be here Wednesday with all of my stuff, but I have all the important things with me."

"So you're storing some stuff here?" I asked, confused.

She put the box down carefully and finally came to stand toe to toe with me. "Yes and no," she hedged. "I was kind of hoping that offer you wanted to make to come live with you was still open."

Still open? "It never closed," I said in a voice hoarse with emotion. "If you're telling me you're moving in, you're going to make me a very happy man. Please tell me that's your plan."

Hell, I didn't want to get ahead of myself, but I couldn't figure out what else she might be doing.

"I'm moving in," she said readily. "I love you, Leo, and I see absolutely no reason to waste another moment. I'd rather be with you for whatever time we're given than to be careful for the rest of my life. I want our future if we have one, Leo. If you still want me. If you love me like I love you."

Fuck! Didn't she already know she was my everything? Because if there was still any doubt in her mind, I'd squash that shit right now.

"So, you just decided you'd move everything in and see how it goes?" I questioned, elated but still flabbergasted.

She nodded. "I figured once I was in, it would be harder to get rid of me and I'd have more time to prove to you that I'm sure of what I want now."

"Are you?" I asked as I crowded her against one of the large pillars on the front porch.

"Very," she said firmly. "I want you, Leo Lancaster. I love you. You can fight me if you want, but you probably won't get away. I plan to stick to you like glue from now on."

I planted a hand beside her head as I rasped, "Do you have any fucking idea how much I love to hear those words? I think I've been in love with you from the moment I found you crying over the loss of your crippled Bengal tiger."

Her tender heart that she tried so hard to hide had enchanted me from the very beginning.

"Thank God," she breathed out. "I was still afraid that I'd ruined the best thing I'd ever found in my entire life."

I shook my head. "I'm not going anywhere, Macy. I'm stuck like glue, too. We'd be married already if everything had gone my way."

Macy wrapped her arms around my neck. "Somehow, I doubt very much I'll be all that hard to convince."

"Fuck! You know me, Macy. You know I rush things. You shouldn't have told me that," I said, trying to put the brakes on my instincts.

I'd have a bloody ring on her finger tomorrow if that's how she felt.

"I'm ready for anything, handsome," she said in a sultry tone. "I really do love you."

I threaded my fingers into her hair as I looked at her earnest expression. "I hope so, because I'll never be able to let you go now."

"I'll never ask you to," she whispered as she pulled my head down.

I kissed her like it was the first and last kiss we'd ever get in our entire lifetime.

Her tongue tangled with mine as we tried to say so many things with that embrace that we couldn't quite express in words.

Love.

Respect.

Need.

Desire.

And an unholy hunger to be a lot closer than we were right now.

"Up," I said gruffly once I'd released her mouth.

She lifted her legs and wrapped them around my waist like she needed me as much as I needed her, which I doubted was even possible.

If I didn't get my cock inside her in the next minute or so, I wasn't sure I'd survive the pounding urgency to claim her.

"I can't wait any longer," I growled into her ear as I carried her inside and locked the door behind me.

"My stuff," she said, sounding more needy than concerned.

"After," I insisted. "It's not like I have neighbors."

I knew I wasn't going to make it to the bedroom, so I dropped her gorgeous ass on the small kitchen table while I trailed kisses down her neck.

"Leo," she moaned as she leaned her head back to give me whatever I wanted.

That capitulation tore at my fucking heart because I sensed that she'd finally decided to trust me with her body and her heart.

Our clothes came off in a frenzy of moving legs, arms and garments tossed to the floor.

"I love you, Macy," I told her huskily as I wrapped my arms around her soft, curvy, gorgeously naked body.

"I love you, Leo Lancaster," she said like it was her vow.

"Shit! Condom!" I growled.

She shook her head. "I went on birth control not long after we met. I'm protected."

"I'm clean, sweetheart," I promised.

"Leo," she said softly. "I know you'd never do anything to hurt me."

"Never," I confirmed.

She fisted her hands in my hair as she demanded, "Then fuck me, Leo. We've both waited long enough."

She wrapped her legs tightly around my waist, and because I couldn't wait another fucking moment, I surged inside her moist, wet heat.

"Fuck! You feel so damn good," I told her as her core squeezed around my bare cock.

"God, Leo, I love you," Macy moaned.

"I love you, too, baby," I groaned, knowing that even if I heard those words for the rest of my life, it would never be enough.

CHAPTER 29

Macy

THE MOMENT HE'D buried himself inside me, I'd practically seen stars.

Our need for each other was primal and fierce, but I wasn't afraid of that carnality.

It was the way we loved each other.

It was the way we needed each other.

It was…us.

"Yes," I hissed as he thrust harder, deeper, and my entire body shuddered.

I felt consumed.

I felt free.

I felt like I was on fire and no one could put out those flames except Leo.

"Fuck! You make me crazy, Macy," Leo said in a husky, low baritone that went right through me.

I wanted to make him completely insane, just like I felt right now.

He gripped my hips and pummeled harder, faster, like he couldn't get close enough or deep enough.

I understood that frenzied desire, the yearning, the longing, the craving that insisted on being satisfied.

I speared my hands into his hair and kissed him, thrusting my tongue into his mouth and moving it in the same rhythm as the stroking of his cock.

Finally, my body humming with desperate need, I moved back and laid my upper body down on the table.

Leo didn't lessen his grip on my hips, nor did he slow down his pace.

He was like a man possessed and I certainly wasn't about to stop him from finding exactly what he needed.

"You're so damn beautiful," he growled as his eyes devoured me. "You're mine, Macy. Always have been and always will be."

Jesus! There was nothing hotter than Leo Lancaster staking his claim.

"Yours," I agreed. "Just like you're mine. Leo, I want…I need…"

Shit! My orgasm was right there…

"Take what you need, sweetheart. Touch yourself," Leo urged.

The temptation was too great to not do what he asked.

I moved my hand down my belly until I got to my core. I wasn't gentle as I touched my clit with the pressure and urgency I needed to come.

"That's it, baby," Leo crooned in encouragement. "Let go."

"Oh, My God! Leo!" I screamed as I went careening over the edge.

My climax rolled over me hard, and it rocked my entire being.

I spasmed fiercely around Leo's cock, but he kept driving into me with a strength that kept my orgasm going for way longer than it should have.

I opened my eyes and watched as Leo groaned my name and found his own release.

For a moment, the only sound around us was the harshness of our breathing as we came down from the madness.

Leo pulled me up and wrapped his arms protectively around my body.

I wrapped my arms around him as he simply held me like he was never going to let me go.

"I love you, baby," he said fiercely.

I laid my head on his shoulder. "I love you, too. It seems like there were a million things I wanted to say to you. Now, I'm speechless. You love me. I love you. We're together. None of the other details really seem to matter right now."

"Now that we're together, the other things don't matter," he grumbled.

"There is the little I'm American and you're British issue," I said, even though I knew even that wasn't a big deal.

We'd find a way to work things out.

"Not an issue," he answered. "Unless you're totally against spending some time in England. We'll probably need to travel back and forth."

"I wouldn't mind that at all unless my boss has a problem with it," I teased.

"Your boss," he said in a husky tone. "Would let you do absolutely anything that made you happy."

"You make me happy, Leo," I told him.

"Then we'll figure out a way to be together most of the time since I already know I'll be a complete prick if I'm not with you," he informed me. "Being away from you all these weeks except for work made me half crazy. I guarantee I won't do well if we have to spend long periods of time apart."

"I don't want that, either," I told him. "I'd rather be together, which is why I'm ditching my apartment. It makes no sense to be apart when we're living in the same area."

"I completely agree. Are you missing Newport Beach?" he asked. "I could buy—"

"No," I answered. "I don't need a place there anymore, Leo. We can visit, but my future is with you, wherever we need or want to be. Whether it's in England or here in Palm Springs. I wouldn't complain if you wanted to take a real vacation once in a while with no work involved. There're so many places I'd like to see and things I'd like to do with you."

"We'll make time," Leo said firmly.

"You inspire me to want to do more than work," I teased him. "I guess I was just waiting for you so we could discover new things together."

"I think I've always been waiting for you," Leo said solemnly. "Once Damian found Nicole, maybe that sparked the possibility that there might be someone out there for me. I can't say that I don't love my work, but it really was a lonely existence. There was something missing, but I quickly discovered that not any woman was going to fill that void. It had to be you, and you certainly took your sweet time before you finally showed up."

"What made you so sure that woman was me?" I lifted my head to look into his gorgeous eyes.

"The crazy connection we have, the intense chemistry. I've never felt this way about another woman, Macy. I knew it didn't happen every day. Granted, I thought Damian was insane for all the crazy things he did to try to win Nicole's heart, but I understood it once I met you. There wasn't much I wasn't willing to do if it meant we'd end up together at the end."

"I'm sorry I made things harder than they should have been for us," I murmured as I buried my face in his neck. "I've actually thought you were the hottest man I'd ever seen since the day I started watching your documentaries. I knew who you were long before you discovered me. I thought you were gorgeous and absolutely fearless."

"Are you going to tell me that you felt that connection when you saw those horrible documentaries?" he asked jokingly.

"No," I said, drawing out the word. "But I might have had a little hero worship crush going on for a while. Little did I know back then that I'd actually get the chance to meet you in person someday. You never noticed how tongue-tied I was when we met at the wedding?"

"Not at all," he said smoothly. "I was too busy trying to control my fascination with you."

"You're crazy," I murmured against his bare skin. "Every single woman at the wedding was ogling you, and you decided to focus on me?"

"I didn't notice their ogling, nor did I care," he answered good-naturedly.

I thought about that for a moment and I was instantly convinced that it was true.

Leo didn't notice when every female eye in the area was on him.

The guy didn't have a vain bone in his body, which was probably a good thing since he was physically perfect.

He stroked my hair as he asked, "How long are you going to make me wait before you'll marry me?"

I lifted my head and looked at him as I said, "I don't remember you even asking me if I wanted to marry you, but if you do, here's a newsflash: I'm going to say yes."

There was no reason for me to tell Leo anything else but the truth. I wanted to be with him for the rest of my life.

He took my head between his hands and looked me in the eye as he queried, "Marry me, Macy?"

My heart stuttered as I looked at the raw vulnerability on his face. "You already know that's a yes."

"We'll go get you a ring tomorrow," he said with a grin.

"I'm not in a huge hurry for that," I informed him.

"I am," he insisted. "It's not official without a ring and I want to see my ring on your finger."

Seriously? Like he needed to worry about some other guy stealing me away from him? Yeah, that wasn't happening.

"I have to be honest," I said. "Just the thought of a big wedding like Nicole's makes me break out in hives."

"Then we'll do something different," he said nonchalantly. "Vegas. A courthouse. A really small service. It doesn't matter to me, Macy."

"I think your family would mind," I said in an exasperated voice. "I'm sure your mom will expect there to be something similar to Nic's wedding."

"I doubt that," he said drily. "She knows me. I don't put a lot of importance on society's expectations. Mum would be happy just to see me married. Take my word on that. I don't think she thought it would ever happen."

"But what if she doesn't—"

"Sweetheart," he interrupted. "This wedding isn't about my family or friends. It's about us. You're the bride, you can have whatever you want."

"Let me think about it," I said.

The last thing I wanted was to piss anyone off, but if I had my way, we'd get married without a lot of fuss.

"Take your time, and don't let Mum's nagging about grandchildren get to you," he advised.

"Kids?" I squeaked. "Do you want to have children? I'm thirty-three years old, Leo."

"And you have plenty of time to think about it," he added smoothly as he picked me up, forcing me to wrap my legs tightly around his waist.

"What are you doing?" I squealed happily as he started to carry me toward the bedroom.

"I think it's time for some distraction," he insisted as he dropped me onto his bed gently.

The bedroom lights were on, which made it very easy for me to ogle his droolworthy body.

My heart stuttered as Leo came down on top of me.

"We'll have to talk about kids eventually," I said, already getting distracted.

Our eyes locked as he said calmly, "We can have children…or not. I'm okay either way, Macy. I have you, and that's really all that matters. Honestly, I'd like to just focus on us for a while."

I wanted the same thing.

One step at a time.

I wrapped my arms around his neck. "And what exactly would you like to discuss right now?"

He grinned. "I think I'd rather show you how much I've missed you over the last several weeks. Is there anything you brought with you that can't survive outside for the next few hours?"

I smiled back at him and sighed.

There was no possible way I could say *no* to that kind of diversion. The stuff I'd left outside would be fine for a few hours.

"We can get it later. Show me, Leo," I insisted.

It was morning before we finally got around to hauling my stuff inside, and by that time I was so distracted that I wasn't worried about anything at all.

EPILOGUE

Macy

Two Years Later...

"HE'S SO ADORABLE," I told Nicole as I reluctantly handed her newborn son back to her. Leo and I had scrambled to get to London the moment we heard that Ethan Charles Lancaster was ready to make his appearance in the world.

Kylie and Dylan had already been in London, and we'd all waited anxiously at the hospital until we knew both mother and son were healthy and safe. We were staying with Kylie and Dylan so we could be in London, but we had purchased a home closer to the conservation center so we could be comfortable when we were in the UK.

It was the perfect ending to an absolutely amazing two years of being a part of the Lancaster family.

With Bella's assistance, Leo and I had been married in a small ceremony at her estate just a few weeks after Leo had asked me to be his wife.

Dylan and Kylie had married a little over a month later in a larger affair that had taken place in London.

We saw Kylie and Dylan a little more often than Damian and Nicole because the former traveled to the States for Kylie's business, but we all got together as much as possible.

It took a little planning, but it wasn't exactly difficult to hop in a private jet and fly across the pond to see my best friends.

I'd soon discovered that Leo's enormous wealth made almost anything possible, and he never hesitated to use that money to take us to places we could explore together.

For the most part, Leo did stay out of field work and focused on the important work he had to do at his conservation centers. However, we had done a few explorations together, and each discovery had a special place in my heart.

We worked hard at both of the conservation centers, but we never forgot to make sure we were taking care of each other and our relationship.

"Two more months and we'll be seeing another newborn Lancaster," Leo said to Dylan as we all stayed seated in the living room while Nicole went to feed her son.

Dylan's face turned pale as he looked at his pregnant wife next to him.

Kylie was expecting to deliver their girl in about eight more weeks.

"I'm not sure I want to see Kylie in that kind of pain," Dylan said, sounding a little nervous.

"I'm not sure you have any choice in the matter," Leo informed him.

"I'm not carrying this little girl any longer than I have to," Kylie said emphatically. "I'm already over the gymnastics routine she's trying to do in my belly. I'm not the least bit afraid of the pain of childbirth. Once it's over, I'll have my daughter."

Dylan pulled his wife close to his side as they sat on the couch together. "I think one child is enough," he grumbled. "She'll have her cousin Ethan to play with."

"Agreed," Damian said from his chair.

"Does Nic get any say in that decision?" Kylie asked with a laugh.

"Of course," Damian said. "So I suppose I'll have to be persuasive in my argument for an only child."

"Cousins are just as good as having a sibling," Dylan commented.

Kylie smiled. "I might be inclined to agree with you."

"I'd always vote for more," Bella said happily from her chair.

Damian lifted a brow. "Really, Mum? You're already getting two in the space of a few months."

"I'm not complaining," she clarified. "I just think there's always room for more."

I leaned in close to Leo as we sat next to each other on the loveseat and said under my breath, "Maybe she'll get another."

We hadn't told anyone, but I'd stopped birth control the month before. Leo and I had decided we wanted a child, and we were hoping we'd eventually get our wish.

If it didn't happen, neither of us would be completely devastated because we were just happy to have each other, but we were both hopeful.

Leo pulled me closer and dropped a gentle kiss to my forehead as he said quietly, "I'm more than happy to keep doing my best to make it happen."

"I'm sure you will," I said with a laugh.

Our gazes locked and my heart tripped because I knew exactly how hard Leo was willing to try.

In fact, he never missed an opportunity.

If effort was a factor, I wouldn't be surprised if I was already pregnant.

I leaned back against Leo and let out a sigh of contentment.

My life was already full simply because I was part of this tight-knit family.

Everyone else continued to banter with each other as Leo asked, "What was that huge sigh about? Are you alright, sweetheart?"

That was Leo.

Always checking on me. Always making sure I was okay.

"I'm fine," I assured him.

Occasionally, I still had surreal moments like this when I wondered how I had gotten lucky enough to have a man like Leo and a family like the one surrounding me now.

The difference was that I was no longer waiting for the other shoe to drop.

I wasn't waiting for the worst to happen.

I was enjoying every single moment because I knew exactly how good my life was now.

"You're smiling. What are you thinking about?" Leo said in a low voice next to my ear.

I turned to him, my smile widening as my mind turned to a much hotter subject. "You, our family and baby making," I teased.

He grinned. "The last one is definitely the most interesting."

I put my arms around his neck as I whispered, "Then we'll have to explore the subject more in depth a little later. I love you, Leo."

"I love you, Macy," he said in a quiet, husky voice right before he kissed me.

His embrace was brief, but the intensity in his eyes told me everything I needed to know.

He loved me.

He needed me.

And we'd definitely be making an attempt or two or three at making a baby as soon as possible.

My smile grew a little wider and I held his gaze for just a little longer so my husband would know that I knew exactly what he was thinking.

"Later," he said in a low, sexy baritone.

Nearly breathless with anticipation, I said, "Not too much later, I hope. I did a little shopping in London for some mood booster knickers. I think you'll like the ones I'm wearing."

"Baby, that's just cruel," he said with a low groan. "I'll make you pay for this one."

"I can't wait," I whispered back, knowing he'd only make me pay in the most pleasurable of ways, and that I'd enjoy every single moment of it just as soon as he could politely drag me off to a bedroom.

He did.

I did.

And it was absolutely sublime.

The End

Please visit me at:
http://www.authorjsscott.com
http://www.facebook.com/authorjsscott

You can write to me at
jsscott_author@hotmail.com

You can also tweet
@AuthorJSScott

Please sign up for my Newsletter for updates, new releases and exclusive excerpts.

Books by J. S. Scott:

Billionaire Obsession Series
The Billionaire's Obsession~Simon
Heart of the Billionaire
The Billionaire's Salvation
The Billionaire's Game
Billionaire Undone~Travis
Billionaire Unmasked~Jason
Billionaire Untamed~Tate
Billionaire Unbound~Chloe
Billionaire Undaunted~Zane
Billionaire Unknown~Blake
Billionaire Unveiled~Marcus
Billionaire Unloved~Jett
Billionaire Unwed~Zeke

Billionaire Unchallenged~Carter
Billionaire Unattainable~Mason
Billionaire Undercover~Hudson
Billionaire Unexpected~Jax
Billionaire Unnoticed~Cooper
Billionaire Unclaimed~Chase

British Billionaires Series
Tell Me You're Mine
Tell Me I'm Yours
Tell Me This Is Forever

Sinclair Series
The Billionaire's Christmas
No Ordinary Billionaire
The Forbidden Billionaire
The Billionaire's Touch
The Billionaire's Voice
The Billionaire Takes All
The Billionaire's Secret
Only A Millionaire

Accidental Billionaires
Ensnared
Entangled
Enamored
Enchanted
Endeared

Walker Brothers Series
Release
Player
Damaged

The Sentinel Demons
The Sentinel Demons: The Complete Collection
A Dangerous Bargain
A Dangerous Hunger
A Dangerous Fury
A Dangerous Demon King

The Vampire Coalition Series
The Vampire Coalition: The Complete Collection
The Rough Mating of a Vampire (Prelude)
Ethan's Mate
Rory's Mate
Nathan's Mate
Liam's Mate
Daric's Mate

Changeling Encounters Series
Changeling Encounters: The Complete Collection
Mate Of The Werewolf
The Dangers Of Adopting A Werewolf
All I Want For Christmas Is A Werewolf

The Pleasures of His Punishment
The Pleasures of His Punishment: The Complete Collection
The Billionaire Next Door
The Millionaire and the Librarian
Riding with the Cop
Secret Desires of the Counselor
In Trouble with the Boss
Rough Ride with a Cowboy
Rough Day for the Teacher
A Forfeit for a Cowboy
Just what the Doctor Ordered
Wicked Romance of a Vampire

The Curve Collection: Big Girls and Bad Boys Series
The Curve Collection: The Complete Collection
The Curve Ball
The Beast Loves Curves
Curves by Design

Writing as Lane Parker
Dearest Stalker: Part 1
Dearest Stalker: A Complete Collection
A Christmas Dream
A Valentine's Dream
Lost: A Mountain Man Rescue Romance

A Dark Horse Novel w/ Cali MacKay
Bound
Hacked

Taken By A Trillionaire Series
Virgin for the Trillionaire by Ruth Cardello
Virgin for the Prince by J.S. Scott
Virgin to Conquer by Melody Anne
Prince Bryan: Taken By A Trillionaire

Other Titles
Well Played w/Ruth Cardello

Printed in Great Britain
by Amazon